The dark waite[...] of evil. The h[...] with the dead. [...] that opened int[...] waiting for hi[...] mortal to comprehend. The deaths that had occurred here were a testament to the evil that embraced darkness like a long lost friend. The dark seemed to creep beneath the door as he gingerly pushed inward, thinking about all that had led to this moment, a moment when he would have to come face to face with something evil in the darkness at Hopkins House.

There is an ancient myth that says when a particularly violent act that leads to death occurs in a house, the parties involved in that act are trapped in perpetuity within the walls of the home, and as time passes these spirits begin to recent intrusions by the living into their world of darkness that envelopes them like a warm blanket on a cold night.

Hopkins House is a converted brownstone in lower Manhattan that sits on a street of broken dreams, where those who have been relegated to the fringes of society forage for their daily bread, unaware of the evil that lurks within their midst.

The Hopkins family left their lavish Manhattan mansion in 1898, when they decided to go west in order to seek greater fortune. Then, they returned when their dreams were obliterated, along with the rest of San Francisco, in the 1906 earthquake. In a few years, the entire family was dead as a result of violent murders, but they did not rest quietly, because during the next 60 years there were many who encountered something evil in the darkness at Hopkins House.

ABOUT THE AUTHOR

Living in a small town (Asheboro, North Carolina), where there was very little for someone with an active imagination to do, Wayne Frye spent much of his childhood writing short stories and movie scripts that simply gathered dust over the years. His first foray into professional writing was in the political genre with the 1971 book, *The Loss of the American Dream*. In 1976, he wrote the screenplay and directed *Simba*, an experimental film that became a popular cult classic on college campuses and cable access channels. He spent many years as a college professor and administrator, concentrating on writing text books. He has also been a television producer and director, specializing in educational and distance learning programming. In 1993, under a pseudonym, he wrote his first fictional work, *The Fall from Apocalypse*.

In 2003, after spending many years directing an intensive academic support program for ghetto children in South-central Los Angeles, he immigrated to an idyllic Canadian island (Vancouver Island) in search of what he calls a more equalitarian, just and compassionate society. He and his wife live in the small seaside community of Ladysmith, British Columbia where they build and restore Victorian homes.

He is Executive Director of the Che4Freedom Foundation (www.che4freedom.50megs.com), which is an organization dedicated to unionizing the world's workers in their fight against globalization and corporate malfeasance. He does all his writing at his beloved *Bay View Chateau*, high on a mountain overlooking the Pacific.

OTHER BOOKS BY J. WAYNE FRYE

TEXTBOOKS
1. *Introduction to Advertising*
2. *Promotions Workbook*
3. *Mastering Marketing Research*
4. *Advertising Design*
5. *Guide to Local Radio-Television Copywriting*
6. *Marketing Plan Workbook*
7. *Public Relations Workbook*

FICTION
1. *The Fall From Apocalypse*
2. *Armageddon Now*
3. *Something Evil in The Darkness at Hopkins House*

NON-FICTION
1. *The Loss of the American Dream*
2. *Cataclysmic Dreams in Black and White*
3. *The Catastrophic Calamities of a Village Idiot*
4. *Guide to Alternative Education*

SOMETHING EVIL IN THE DARKNESS AT HOPKINS HOUSE

by

J. Wayne Frye

10 9 8 7 6 5 4 3 2 1

Copyright 2006
by
J. Wayne Frye

All rights reserved. No part of this book may be reproduced or transmitted in any form or by any other means, electronic or mechanical, including photocopying, recording, or by any information storage and retrieval system, without permission from the author.

Catalogue Number: 20065186208

ISBN: 0-9735973-4-8

Manufactured in Canada

Peninsula Publishing / Colony Publishing
Distributes Books Under the Following Labels:
Adams Books   Incredible Stories   Australian Literary Classics
Canadian Literary Classics   Fireside Books   Olympia Books

Additional copies of this book may be ordered in the currencies listed on the back from the below address. Add 20% shipping/handling for Canadian and U.S. orders, 30% for shipment outside of North America.

**Fireside Books
Distribution Centre NA
#1 Adams Place
Suite M-16
Victoria, BC V9B 6P6**
Web-site: firesidebooks.1colony.com

TABLE OF CONTENTS

Prologue: Page 7
Manifestation of Evil

Chapter 1: Page 8
Perpetrators of Evil

Chapter 2: Page 15
Hopkins House Beckons

Chapter 3: Page 19
Captive of the Evil in Hopkins House

Chapter 4: Page 27
Ending the Evil That Plagues Hopkins House

Chapter 5: Page 31
A Demon at Play in Hopkins House

Chapter 6: Page 37
Of Mortal Form

Chapter 7: Page 43
Massacre at Hopkins House

Chapter 8: Page 59
Something Cold and Clammy in the Darkness

Chapter 9: Page 67
Harbinger of Darkness

Chapter 10: Page 75
Pain and Evil of the Vilest Form

Chapter 11: Page 89
A Useless Instrument in Hopkins House

Chapter 12: Page 99
Putting the Ghosts of Hopkins House to Rest

Epilogue: Page 127
Rachael

TO: My dear friend Brent, with whom I shared many joyous days during our youth, and who has brought raucous laughter to multitudes by being the subject of *"The Thunder Road Tale."*

PROLOGUE
MANIFESTATION OF EVIL

There is an ancient myth that alleges when a particularly violent act that leads to death occurs in a house, the parties involved in that act can be trapped in perpetuity within the walls of the home, and as time passes these spirits begin to recent intrusions by the living into their world of darkness that envelopes them like a warm blanket on a cold night. These spirits eventually become more brazen until they free themselves from this imprisonment and move about freely within the confines of the home, perpetrating evil acts to drive out those who dare disturb their solitude.

Hopkins House is a converted brownstone in lower Manhattan that sits on a street of broken dreams, where those who have been relegated to the fringes of a society based on greed forage for their daily bread, unaware of the evil that lurks within their midst as they already must deal with the evil promulgated by a society that has no compassion for the poor and downtrodden. At one time, this stately mansion was home to a wealthy baron of excess who ruled a clothing manufacturing empire. Harry Hopkins, his wife and three children were the original residents of Hopkins House, Harry having built it in his 40th year as a testament to the wealth and power he had achieved as head of a company that operated sweat shops to supply fine clothing to America's upper classes.

In 1898, Harry moved his family to San Francisco, when he found he could pay even lower wages by exploiting Chinese immigrants willing to work for less than he was paying the Irish in New York. The move proved a folly when the 1906 earthquake nearly obliterated the city. Deciding to move back to New York, Harry and his family returned to Hopkins House, where the evil incubated, grew and spread like a Middle Age's plague in a home that seemed to lovingly embrace the unmitigated evil like it was an old, dear and revered friend.

CHAPTER 1
PERPETRATORS OF EVIL

It was nearly 2:00 A.M. The elevator was broken again, so Aaron Adams walked the three flights of stairs up to his office. As he climbed the last stair, turned the corner and looked at the door with *Adams Investigations* written in bold black letters on the window, he noticed that a note had been placed in the door jam. Removing the brown envelope, he put the key in the lock, opened the door, turned on the light and tossed the envelope on his desk without giving it a second thought.

He removed his jacket, flopped down on the well-worn sofa and contemplated his life. He had become a moderately successful private investigator, but felt much older than his 35 years. Since returning from Vietnam, as a decorated war hero, almost 13 years ago, his life had been one of turmoil. He had hated the war, but like so many other poor youths, he was sent to defend America from the evil communists while the children of the rich and privileged got college deferments or hid in the National Guard. For a brief time he had worked with Vietnam Veterans Against the War, but decided that a society that spent more on war than on alleviating human misery was too corrupt to ever change. He gave up and elected to make his way in an uncaring society the best way he could. He apprenticed with the well-known Queens private eye, Harold Wingate, then after three years, set up his own agency in lower Manhattan. He had spent years working in the underbelly of a society that was corrupt, arrogant, uncaring and unsympathetic to the needs of the less fortunate. Now, he was trying to decide what to do with the rest of his life. He was tired, dead tired and exhausted from peeping into people's lives and seeing the very worst of humanity. The weariness was overwhelming him. Only last year, the country had elected Ronald Reagan President, and he knew that the misery of the poor would only increase as the "boob from Hollywood" handed the country over to the corporate thieves who would rape and plunder in pursuit of their avaricious need to possess more and more.

   Each day, as he moved among the scurrying masses who were trying to keep their heads above water in a country with no heart or mercy, he longed to escape to a more equalitarian and just society. Yet, he was a slave to the same rat race as everyone else. Although he eschewed the manifestations of the capitalist lifestyle, he, too, was like so many others, forced to become part of a system he abhorred. He worried about making enough to pay his rent, his gas bill, his phone bill and his medical expenses. He reflected on how the white man arrived in America and thought he had brought civilization to the heathen Indians. What hypocrisy. Before the white man showed up, the concept of ownership was foreign to the natives, who had an abundance of what they needed to survive. The forests and plains of America teemed with bountiful crops and game that provided the sustenance of life, and the natives shared what they had, so that no one went hungry. The land was not fenced off so the few could keep the many from sharing in the wealth. The earth was abundant and plentiful. Now, the rich walled themselves up in enclaves of opulence while the poor were isolated in the ghettos of misery and despair. All the while, this banal affront to humanity was acclaimed to be the salvation of mankind. Aaron was tired, so tired. He closed his eyes, eased back on the sofa and fell into a deep sleep.

   When the morning sun's rays filtered through the blinds, Aaron blinked a few times, wiped the fogginess from his eyes and got up to go into the corner bathroom for a quick shower and a change of clothes. He often wondered why he bothered to keep an apartment, because most of his sleeping and showering was done at the office. In fact, this was his life. The confines of a 12 by 15 office, a small anti-chamber and bathroom had become his whole world. He felt confined, as if he was imprisoned by a world that was rapidly isolating him. He sighed with resignation, realizing that he had to face another day in the armpits of a city of broken dreams.

After showering and changing clothes, Aaron forlornly sat behind his desk, propped his feet up, and eyed the brown envelope that still lay unopened next to the desk lamp. He quizzically wondered what it contained, but for some reason he had trepidation about opening it. It was as if something was telling him to toss it into the trash can, and forget that he had ever seen it. A dread crept over him as he slowly reached for it with a sweaty left hand that quivered as he picked it up. The envelope was cold, so cold it sent a chill through to the bone. Wiping his brow with his right hand, he held the envelope in his hand, still contemplating what to do.

Moaning slightly, Aaron slowly pulled back the lightly clued tab, noticed that it had a courier stamp on the back at the center of the seal, and removed an equally cold piece of embossed pink stationery and began to read:

19 February, 1984

Dear Mr. Adams:

Although we have never met, I have inquired about your integrity, and I have been assured you are a man of utmost discretion and trustworthiness. I would appreciate it if you would come to Hopkins House at 3718 Farragut Avenue in Lower Manhattan at 8:00 P.M. tomorrow night to discuss a matter of utmost importance. I shall look forward to meeting you in person.

Sincerely,

Rachael Hopkins

What a strange letter thought Aaron. Rachael Hopkins was a name unfamiliar to him, but he knew the area where Hopkins House was located, a desolate part of Lower Manhattan that was near Skid Row.

Reading the mysterious communication once more, Aaron pondered what Rachael Hopkins wanted from a private investigator. He let his mind wonder, trying to picture what this mysterious woman might be like. She wrote the letter yesterday, so she would expect him tonight.

He spent the day reviewing the Blount case which would require his court testimony next week, but his anticipation of meeting Rachael Hopkins kept interfering with his concentration. Before he realized it, the old 1950's clock above the door was at 7:00 P.M. Pulling out an IRT schedule, he saw there was an express subway at 7:10 that would get him near Hopkins House, but he would have to take a taxi from the train station to Farragut Avenue. As he closed his door, turned the lock and peered through the blurred glass window, he noticed the brown envelope and stationery as it fluttered lightly out the open window. Yet, none of the other papers on his desk even rustled in the cold, damp night air.

Getting off the subway at Euclid and Broadway, Aaron sauntered through the station trying to avoid eye contact with the helpless souls who huddled against the tile walls in the only refuge they had from the cold. Yet, he could not avoid a few who pleaded with outstretched hands for some type of compassion from a fellow human being. Reaching in his pocket and parting with a few quarters, dimes and nickels, he could not help but think that in Albany and Washington, DC, the politicians who were supposed to represent these people were probably dining on caviar and filet mignon. Why could the people of America not see that everyone, but a chosen few, was only a pay check or two from being in the same predicament? As he glided up the debris-strewn stairs, he smelled the stench of poverty and sensed the pain of those relegated to the fringes of a society that had no sympathy. This place of agony and anxiety was the direct result of a society based on greed, a society so sick and perverted that it had long ago lost its moral compass as it turned its back on fairness and compassion.

Exiting the station, Aaron looked about at trash piled high on the streets and sidewalks as a few cars whisked by, blowing debris into the curbs. He thought that you would see nothing like this in the suburbs of Connecticut or the lower Hudson, where the rich hid behind their gated estates to avoid the squalor of the city created by their own avaricious and greedy lifestyles. All this was the direct result of the rich preying on the poor, taking advantage of those they deemed unworthy of the good life. Sometimes Aaron seethed with unadulterated hatred for capitalism and all the pain it caused to the less fortunate. He often harkened back to his days in Vietnam, where he was told that he had to defend the American way. Was this the reason for which he was sent to Vietnam to kill the yellow man? Was he supposed to kill communists to preserve a society that sanctioned gross inequity by exploiting and demonizing poverty as if it was some type of disease that must be quarantined to protect the rich so they did not have to deal with it?

A Yellow Cab eased to the curb as Aaron signalled the driver to stop. The antiquated Checker automobile was as worn out as the neighbourhood. The driver, a dark, chubby man with two front teeth missing, smiled and nodded his head.

"Where to, sir?"

As the cumbersome, old vehicle chortled forward, Aaron said, "You know where Hopkins House is on Farragut?"

The driver slammed on the brakes, turned to Aaron and shook his head vehemently, "I'll take you to the corner of Farragut and Broadway, but I ain't going nowhere near Hopkins House."

"O.K., I can use a little exercise, but what is the problem with Hopkins House?"

"You ain't ever heard the stories about Hopkins House? People just don't go there, if 'un they got any sense."

"Do you know the Hopkins family?"

The driver looked in the rear view mirror, shook his head and said, "Fellow, you ain't ever heard about Hopkins House?"

"Well, I have heard the name Hopkins many times, but only in reference to Mark Hopkins in California and the hotel in San Francisco that bears his name. I did run into a few people named Hopkins when I was at Fort Bragg in North Carolina during the war. I even dated a girl one weekend named Hopkins when I went to Denton, North Carolina with a buddy I made in basic training. They were a well-respected family. I am not aware of any New York Hopkins, though."

"Sir, I don't know nothing about no North Carolina Hopkins family, but I do know about this family, and they ain't very well respected at all. In fact, I think they's all dead. But being dead don't mean they ain't still around."

"What does that mean?"

"Just what I said. Just because some people are dead, don't mean they ain't still around. That house is evil. Ain't nobody goes nowhere near it, day or night. The bums on the street or the homeless people will not even sit on the stoop. They's been too many things happen to people that been in or near that house. If you take my advice, you will have me turn around and take you back to the subway station, and forget about going to Hopkins House."

"You ever met Rachael Hopkins?"

"Can't say that I have, sir. I ain't ever been near the place, except one time when I dropped a well-dressed gentleman off at the front stoop. He told me to wait. I saw him go up to the door and some gorgeous lady in a long black cloak opened the door. She looked at me, with the darkest eyes I ever seen. I never seen much of her face. But those eyes, those eyes burned like the fires of hell. I felt like they was looking right through me into the depths of my soul. I decided I wasn't waiting for nobody. They could call a cab later. I hauled ass outta there, and I never looked back. I had heard tales about the place, but I never believed until the night I saw that evil looking creature open the door. Ain't been back on the street since, and I ain't never gonna go back. That's a fact if there ever was one."

Stopping at Broadway and Farragut, Aaron paid the cabbie and looked down the short street that dead ended about 300 metres away. After peering through the moonlight into the black shadows beyond, Aaron thought he discerned an eerie glow coming from a three story house on the right side at the end of the street.

Aaron listened to the faint sounds of traffic that was nearby, but seemed far away. It was as if the sounds were muffled by the darkness. There were no lights on the street, and the dilapidated buildings all appeared to be deserted, except for the faint light that came from the aforementioned house.

Although an extremely courageous man, Aaron could not help a slight feeling of apprehension concerning the forthcoming meeting with Rachael Hopkins. He pulled back his top coat, unbuttoned his jacket and reached inside his coat to pull out the death dealer. The big bastard of a 45 was the great equalizer that had often given him a sense of security when he faced unknown danger. Even though he knew it was loaded and ready, force of habit made him flip open the chamber, just to make sure. You never went into battle without being sure you were ready. Yet, he was still unsure of what he was about to face. Was his dread unfounded? Had he just been the victim of his own active imagination or was he about to face something truly sinister in the imposing house at the end of the street. He did not believe in ghosts, but he certainly believed in the evil that one man could perpetrate on another.

CHAPTER 2
HOPKINS HOUSE BECKONS

The darkness on Farragut Street appeared to close in around Aaron. As he walked briskly toward the end of the street, the cold air felt as if it was slapping him in the face. The steady stream of fog coming out of his mouth seemed to float skyward, taking the shape of a ghostly spectre. He stopped about a third of the way down the street, just to contemplate what he was doing.

A few years ago, he had been in a war. He had often experienced the approaching calamity of battle with a tingling up and down his spine and flushness in his face. That feeling was back now, as he sensed a great uneasiness about Hopkins House. His breathing became shallow and laboured, as he just stood near the curb looking, looking at the stoop down the street that led into Hopkins House. The stairs seemed to be contracting and expanding, almost beckoning for him to continue his journey into the unknown. Yet, he was extremely apprehensive. Even the war had not had this effect on him. Aaron was scared. Yes, he could admit it. He was scared, but of what?

He began to sweat in the cold night air. He looked at the dilapidated buildings around him, and they began to swirl in his mind. Dark and foreboding, each building appeared to harbour its own evil. Yet, Hopkins House continued to beckon, but Aaron's feet seemed clued to the pavement, his mind racing with thoughts of what awaited at the end of the darkness that engulfed him.

Aaron heard a faint noise. Turning his head slightly to his right without moving his feet, he noticed a small light seeming to emanate from between two partially broken boards that covered a basement window in the old brownstone behind him. There was complete quiet except for slight whispering noises.

Aaron walked slowly toward the opening between the two boards. Peering in the window he saw a short, thin, probably handsome man, maybe 40 years old, as he stood above a discarded mattress. The only light was a flashlight that lay on the floor beside the mattress, casting an eerie glow against the back wall. He could only see the man from the side, as the light seemed to almost make him out as a caricature that stood there with his penis erect, and his right hand placed on the shaft. On the mattress, completely naked was a young woman of maybe 20 with her legs spread wide, and a generous amount of dark, black pubic hair. Why, why was Aaron perspiring in the cold night air?

The mind is an instrument of recollection, and Aaron recalled the time, as a young boy, that he had come home from school early, and was delighted to see that his father was home. His mother always worked late, but an early day for his father meant that they would share some good times together, maybe passing the football, or playing with the board hockey game that he loved so much.

Always enjoying the times he shared with his father out in the workshop, he was delighted to see the door to the garage open. It meant that in the back of the garage, where a small door opened into the workshop, he would find his father, probably moving the old mattress out that had been put there a few days before. As he approached the garage, he decided to be very quiet, so he could slip up on his dad and surprise him. As he entered the garage, he heard a voice say, "Don't tease me, let me have some of that beautiful thing."

As he moved to the partially opened door he saw his father, standing above a mattress, and his new secretary lying on it, naked, with her legs spread wide as she smiled at his naked father, urging him to bring the huge member between his legs and plunge it into the root of her passion. His father, with a massive erection, placed his hand on his shaft and smiled.

Aaron turned, ran quietly from the garage, never letting his father know what he had seen.

Why was Aaron now remembering that childhood incident? Why did those images suddenly come back to haunt him? Shaking his head, and blinking his eyes, Aaron continued to peer through the opening. The man suddenly turned his gaze toward Aaron. It was his father. It was his long dead father.

The light went out and the room was bathed in complete darkness. Aaron's heart pounded as he turned and leaned his back against the boards, breathing heavily. Then, from across the street, he thought he saw an image, an outline of some spectre from hell approaching him with a corrupt countenance. The image was like a fog, a fog with faint arms and legs. Yet, even it seemed to be just an outline with no real form. Then he heard music borne from the distance, from the front of Hopkins House. The fog began to glow subdued amber as it glided ever so slowly toward Aaron. He instinctively blinked his eyes, and the vision was gone. Yet, the music continued, a light, smooth sound of a piano emitting from Hopkins House. After a solid steady harmony, it paused and then rose again. There was a sublime mournfulness to the sound, almost as if someone was crying out for solace to ease pain and despair. Each stroke of the keys appeared to be a tear, a tear of loneliness, agony, torture, anxiety and anguish. The sadness almost brought Aaron, himself, to tears as he followed the sounds toward the entrance to Hopkins House. Climbing the stairs, the sound seemed to penetrate to his heart like a dagger buried deep within his rib cage. He had trouble breathing, and stumbled slightly, grabbing the railing to keep from tumbling forward.

Aaron paused at the huge, thick, oak door to Hopkins House. Still enthralled by the music that had a distinct cadence to it, the cadence of a slow, methodical funeral dirge, he pensively stood there on the stoop, hesitating to ring the old pull bell imbedded in the brick.

The front of the house seemed to be alive, almost saying to him, "Enter the cold darkness of Hopkins House." The music halted, and the door knob began to turn, then the door seemed to expand and contract, almost as if the house was beckoning him.

CHAPTER 3
CAPTIVE OF THE EVIL IN HOPKINS HOUSE

As the door opened, Aaron prepared himself to come face to face with an old, bent, scraggly looking woman who, no doubt, needed a private investigator for some nefarious family spying. To his surprise, standing in the doorway was an incredibly beautiful woman in her late 30's. Had he not experienced the earlier horrors on the way to Hopkins House, he would have thought she was about to open the doors to paradise. His sanguine expectations were exceeded in every way. Rachael Hopkins was as graceful looking as a gazelle. She was tall, probably a little overweight, but incredibly sensuous with magnificent curves in all the right places and perky, huge breasts that seemed to be fighting to be freed from the thin silk blouse that she wore. Her eyes were a deep, dark brown, set-off by incredibly long, dark lashes that intensified their colour. Her complexion, although slightly dark, seemed be somewhat anaemic.

"At last Mr. Adams, I am so glad to see you. I was afraid you might not come." She said as she stretched out her hand, and grasped Aaron's.

Noticing her hand was cold, Aaron thought, "Cold hand, warm heart." And, he certainly hoped that he would have an opportunity to see just how warm she was.

"Come in Mr. Adams," said Rachael, as she turned and headed into the dark panelled hallway.

As she moved down the dark hall, Aaron noticed a dim light reflecting from the open doorway of a room to the right. As she passed the door, he could almost see through the thin silk material that tightly hugged her butt. The crack between her cheeks indicated that she was not wearing any panties. Aaron felt an erection start to grow in his pants.

Rachael stopped at the stairs, turned to her left, and pointed into a sitting room with two old, overstuffed sofas, a fireplace and a Queen Anne chair.

"Have a seat Mr. Adams, and I will get you a drink. All I have is some old scotch, 1908, if I recall correctly."

"That would be great. Thank you very much."

Aaron entered the room, but turned to watch her walk down the hall to the far side of the stairs and mumbled, "Damn," when he observed the gentle side to side sway of her hips.

Sitting on one of the sofas that faced each other at right angles to the fireplace, Aaron noticed the fireplace looked like it had not been used in years as the ashes seemed to be crusty and old, with the two small logs left, appearing to have mildew on them. The room appeared to be in a general state of decay, with dust on the tables, and there was a musky smell to the sofa upon which he sat.

There was something else about the room that Aaron could not at first discern, but upon thinking awhile, he realized there was an intense loneliness to the place, almost as if it cried out for companionship. Yet, as he looked at the crusty walls and torn wallpaper, there was also arrogance to the room, a feeling that made him sense that he was imposing on someone's domain.

Looking above the fireplace mantel, he felt the deep, dark set eyes of the man in the picture that hung on the wall, immaculately attired in a turn of the century suit, seeming to stare at him. The eyes had coldness to them, almost to the point of being daggers of ice. Aaron actually felt a chill as the eyes seemed to look right through him. Turning his head to the right, he noticed the windows had thick blue brocade shades that looked like they were from the turn of the century, and the dust was about an inch thick on them.

Rachael came through the doorway, resplendently gorgeous. Aaron's attraction to her was obvious, as his eyes focused on the sensual sway of her hips. She smiled, sat down the large glass of scotch and stood before him with her bra free breasts heaving up and down, the perky nipples sticking through the thin silk blouse. Aaron was on fire with desire, and it seemed that Rachael was almost laughing at him, teasing him with her provocative nature.

"Enjoy your drink Mr. Adams. You may need it after I tell you what I asked you here to do."

The soft illumination of the full moon could be seen through the partially closed drapes. The light reflecting off the coffee table shone between Rachael's slightly parted legs. The thin silk material showed the panty-less outline of a dark mound beneath the material. She obviously had a generous amount of dark pubic hair. The erection in Aaron's pants became almost painful as she sat on the sofa, crossing her legs to show a generous amount of muscular thigh.

"In my business Miss Hopkins, I am rarely shocked."

"Do you believe in ghosts Mr. Adams," said Rachael as she turned toward Aaron, exposing more of her thigh, and smiling broadly, showing glistening white teeth.

"Well, I believe in what I can see Miss Hopkins, and I have never seen a ghost."

"How do you know? Do you know what a ghost looks like?"

"I can't say that I do."

"Then you may have seen them and not realized it. They would not come out and announce themselves as ghosts. I do not think that would be in their nature."

Aaron's interest was piqued as he leaned forward and said, "Perhaps you should explain the nature of what you desire from me."

"First, I must relate to you the history of this house Mr. Adams. It is a very sordid tale filled with nefarious and cruel characters, many of whom had extremely evil intentions while alive, and, I believe, even more evil intentions after their deaths. I have lived in this house for many years. I have seen things that would make most people cringe with fear, run out the front door and never return. Yet, as the last in a long line of Hopkins I have endured that which is often unendurable. I have seen that which is unbelievable. I have felt the evil in this house, and I have vowed to rid it of that evil, no matter how long it takes. Yet, I am ignorant of one very important fact, and I need a man of your talents on the outside to find out for me the truth behind all that makes the Hopkins name synonymous with evil in this city. I must put to rest once and for all the evil that permeates the walls of this den of the devil."

After a prolonged silence, Aaron shook his head, smiled and said, "Miss Hopkins, I am a man who is afraid of very little. I have seen war, war in Vietnam, where life was cheaper than a drop of water. I have seen men reduced to their basest animal instincts. I have seen Americans torture prisoners in ways that are too sinister for most people to comprehend. I have seen the arrogance of power as practiced by those who send men out to die in exercises of futility. I have watched the evil perpetrated by politicians like Ronald Reagan who have no compassion for the average person. I have watched as America calls others evil while America, itself, practices the vilest form of evil by allowing people to go without healthcare, live in squalid ghettos while the rich wall themselves off in palatial estates protected by a system of institutionalized greed, and I have seen our country spend billions on bombs and guns while the people beg for a piece of bread. I do not fear the evil of those who are dead. The evil I fear comes from those who are alive."

"I certainly see your point, Mr. Adams, and I agree wholeheartedly. You are sitting in a home built by a baron of greed who got wealthy off the poor who toiled in his sweat shops. Yet, there is some evil that continues after death. The evil of Ronald Reagan, for example, will continue long after he is gone. What he does today, will have an adverse affect on future generations who must pay the debts both socially and fiscally that he will run up by his complete disregard for the less fortune while he lines the pockets of the rich with his tax cuts and obscene spending on defence. Ronald Reagan is an idiot, who acts like a President, but has no real idea of the evil that he is perpetrating. However, the evil here is of a different kind. It has no monetary component. It is much more sinister than that. This evil is all-encompassing, and it continues for generation after generation, for no other reason than the desire to just do evil for evil's sake."

Aaron leaned back on the sofa, enjoying an even better view of Rachael's thigh. "Then please tell me what it is that I can do for you, Miss Hopkins."

"You may call me Rachael, first."

"Fine and I am Aaron, Rachael."

"Then let me begin Aaron with Harry Hopkins, and how he was the initial perpetrator of evil in this doomed house."

"Please do, Rachael."

"Harry Hopkins came to New York City in 1882 to seek his fortune. No one is sure from whence he came, but judging by his accent, all assumed he had migrated from somewhere down south. He had a knack for sewing, so he managed to save enough money to open a small tailor shop on Broadway and Euclid. After a few years he added more and more machines, and soon was turning out a large quantity of clothing."

Aaron shifted his weight slightly, leaning a little closer to Rachael, and he noticed a faint smell of lilacs on her.

"By 1892, he had become very successful, so successful that he built this huge mansion on Farragut. As the wages of his Irish workers got higher, he decided to open a plant in San Francisco, where he could use cheap Chinese immigrant labour. This house was boarded up in 1898, and he moved to San Francisco with his wife, Anna, and his three young daughters; Candace, Charlene and I forget the third one's name, I think it started with an R, no it was an L, her name was Lynn. Anyway, they were, all apparently very happy there, but something strange happened in 1906. Candace, the oldest daughter who was 17, bought an odd looking wooden jewellery box that was 6 inches wide, 6 inches long and 6 inches high. There was a lock on it, but no key, so she bought it without ever opening it. She took it home, and planned to have a locksmith make her a key, but before she could do so, the 1906 earthquake occurred, and their building completely collapsed. Fortunately, they were outside when the quake hit, and the building's collapse did not injure them. They immediately decided to return to New York, but Candace went back into the collapsed building, not searching for anything of value, but for the jewellery box. Harry Hopkins was furious with her and threatened to throw it away when she emerged from the ruins, box in hand. They had a violent argument, and Harry actually struck his daughter."

Aaron interrupted, "And how do you know all this?"

"It is just something that has been passed on to me through the years. It was well-known within the family."

Aaron was intrigued now. "I assume they returned to Manhattan."

"Yes, within a few hours of the earthquake they had managed to procure horses and a wagon. They left for Sacramento."

Aaron was really warming to the story now. "I also assume they took the train back here from Sacramento."

"Yes and the only possession they brought with them was the box Candace had rescued from the ruins of their home. Upon returning, they immediately came to Hopkins House, where they continued their old life, as if they had never left. Harry's business became even more successful, but something sinister began to happen to the family. Each one of them started to change in negative ways. The change was dramatic, so dramatic that it eventually led to murder of the foulest kind."

The word murder seemed to put Rachael in an almost trance like state. She became introspective, as if she was lost in a contemplative suspension of time and place where the past merged with the present, making the two worlds collide in a cornucopia of nefarious and evil intentions.

"Rachael, Rachael," said Aaron has he tried to bring her out of her trance like state.

"I am sorry Aaron. I have not told of these incidents in so long that it just reminds me of the pain and agony that occurred here so many years ago. It is not an easy thing to relate. Knowing that great suffering has been an integral part of this house for so long, only reminds me of what has been lost here. It was more than just lives, it was the beginning of evil, an evil that must finally be put to rest after all these years, or it will continue to grow and spread like a plague on all who dare encroach upon the world of the dead within the walls of this home."

"Rachael, I am an open-minded man and want to understand you, but I refuse to believe that you cannot escape what you perceive as evil within this house. The front door is your ticket to a new life. Simply walk out, and leave all this behind. There are no ghosts here, just memories that play on furtive and impressionable minds. Leave this place. Leave with me, now."

"I wish it were that simple, but it is not. I am a prisoner of the past, and until I locate a certain object that will end the evil, I am unable to leave. That is the reason you are here. Your being here represents the only chance to free myself from the obligations I have to the Hopkins family. When you find what I need, only then will I feel that I can unleash myself from the bonds that inexorably tie me to this house and the ghosts that continue to perpetrate evil from within the confines of this home that harbours the demon of darkness. You see, I am a captive of the evil in Hopkins House."

CHAPTER 4
ENDING THE EVIL THAT PLAGUES HOPKINS HOUSE

Aaron, enamoured and captivated by the lovely Rachael Hopkins, reached out with his right hand and placed it on her folded hands. Giving her a reassuring smile, he squeezed her hand slightly and said, "Tell me what it is I can do Rachael. I am at your disposal, willing to do all I can to ease your pain."

She moved her hands and clasped his right hand in her beautiful, soft, somewhat cold hands, smiling profusely at him as she said, "You are a dear man, and I do think you are the one for whom I have looked for so long to finally bring closure to this mystery. I believe you can tackle the forces of evil and stand tall against adversity that would overwhelm many lesser men."

"Do not inflate my ego too much, Rachael. I am a mere mortal."

"There is a fine line between the mortal and the immortal, believe me, and many times the immortal can pass into the mortal plain with those who are unaware that the dead walk among them. Ghosts are much more than just spectres of the night."

"I will keep that in mind, but I still have no idea of what you wish me to do to assist you."

"Let me finish my story. You must learn of how all this evil started. The key is the aforementioned box which I mentioned. Well, actually, it is what was in the box that is the key to the evil that permeates the very core of this house today. It is an evil that was incubated here, grew over time and eventually destroyed Harry Hopkins and his family in an orgy of bloody violence. The evil began with the purchase of the box, and once it was opened, its contents led to doom for all in this house."

Rachael arose from the sofa, stood in all her glory before Aaron, and said, "Let me get you another drink."

"Sure I would like that."

Watching her walk out of the room was a sensuous experience for Aaron. Each stride seemed to make the tight-clinging, long silk skirt wrap around her voluptuous body, accentuating every curve. The skirt looked like a turn of the century garment that had been used for lounging by the aristocrats of a by-gone era. Aaron thought how wonderful it would be to lounge with this sinewy, epicurean creature wrapped in his masculine arms. The strains of the erection in his pants made him reach down to adjust his manhood and ease the pain of a stiff member that was fighting for release from confinement.

Returning to the room, Rachael smiled at Aaron, almost as if she knew what he was experiencing. Was she enjoying the tease? Did she have any idea of just how sensuous a woman she was? Did she get some sadistic pleasure from torturing men with her salacious actions?

"I brought you a bite to eat Mr. Adams, some crackers and cheese. That is all I have, as I only have food delivered on occasion, and I rarely have guests. I am afraid that I live a very sedate, lonely and quiet life." Said Rachael, as she put the plate and drink on the table in front of Aaron while staring into his eyes, and slightly licking her thick, ruby red lips.

"I am surprised that you do not have a long line of suitors at the door every evening, Rachael. You are obviously an incredibly attractive and appealing woman."

"What a nice thing to say. However, I am afraid I have settled into a very pedestrian lifestyle for many years now. I am a product of a very stodgy upbringing. My parents were very old-fashioned. I have had my wild moments in the past, though."

Rachael's elegant face, her wonderful flowing long black hair and deep dark penetrating eyes made it difficult for Aaron to get his breath, as he sat mesmerized by this magnificent creature. He was bewildered and dazed. It was as if her beauty was growing as they sat across from one another on the sofa. The more he looked, the more magnificent she became, almost as if she was transforming right in front of him. The moonlight continued to penetrate the dimly lit room, making her seem to take on an angelic glow as the moonbeams bounced off her dark coal-black hair while she continued to smile at Aaron.

As Aaron put some cheese on a cracker, he offered it to her, but she shook her head indicating she was not interested in eating. Aaron's thoughts turned to sex. Would she be interested in old-fashioned fornication? Would that be the nourishment she craved? Her manner and body language seemed to cry out for the embrace of a virile man, but dare he risk offending her?

Just as he was about to reach out and embrace her, he was halted with an abrupt, "Let me continue my story Aaron while you eat and drink. I think you will find it most illuminating."

Somewhat disappointed, Aaron replied, "Yes, please go on about the contents of the box."

Without saying a word, she leaned forward, put a piece of cheese on a cracker and handed it to Aaron. There was something deeply earnest and caring in the way she did it, almost as if it was more than just a flirtatious act from an incredibly sensuous woman. It was as if she was saying to Aaron that she accepted him as her confidant, and that she knew he could be trusted with the most intricate of details about her needs and desires. They had moved beyond just a professional relationship. There was now a simpatico that made them both earnest in their desires toward one another. Aaron even felt his erection soften, as if he had moved beyond mere physical attraction to a genuinely sincere, ingenuous understanding.

"What I am about to tell you will be shocking, but in order to understand the importance of your mission Aaron, you must know all the sordid details that have made Hopkins House a place of broken dreams and promises where the ghosts of the past haunt the present day in an intense desire to continue the evil that has incubated and grown into a monstrous, destructive force that longs to embrace those who dare enter this domain."

Rachael reached under the sofa, and she pulled out an old, thick album. She handed it to Aaron, and said, "Within this book is all you need to know about the evil. I need to hire you to find what was in the box. The contents are explained in this album. Only when that item is returned to Hopkins House will the ghosts be put to rest. I must ask you to leave now, because I do not think it wise for you to be here too long. My phone number is in the directory under Hopkins House. If you require an advance in payment, I have the cash here for you now."

"Well, an advance would be nice as I am not known for my financial stability."

Rachael turned leaned forward, pulled out the drawer on the coffee table and removed some $100 bills that seemed to be extremely old and somewhat tattered. She handed the money to Aaron, smiling as she said, "You let me know when you need more, the house is managed by a trust, and I, like you, although it may not seem so, am not financially stable either."

She took Aaron by the arm and led him out of the room and down the hallway to the front door. Standing at the door she moved close enough for Aaron to feel her breasts against his chest. As she opened the door to usher him out, she said, "It is up to you now to assist me in ending the evil that plagues Hopkins House."

CHAPTER 5
A DEMON AT PLAY IN HOPKINS HOUSE

As Aaron walked down the stairs, he glanced back; hoping to get one more look at Rachael, but the house was completely dark. Even the dim porch light had been turned off. This was definitely going to be the strangest case he had ever untaken. With the album tucked under his right arm, he walked down the street, instinctively looking to his left and right to make sure there was no one around. The street was deserted and deathly silent. As he passed the boarded up building where he had seen his vision, he peeped in once more between the boards, but the place was dark. Yet, he felt there was someone watching. The feeling was overpowering, but he continued toward the end of the street as he quickened his pace toward the lights of Broadway. Hailing a cab, he leaned back in the well worn seat, and silently headed toward his office. He was unsure of whether he should open the album or not, as he was not certain he even wanted to take the case, but when the vision of Rachael came into his mind, he knew he was hooked. There was no way, he could let her down.

Climbing the stairs to his office, he was almost hugging the album. He seemed to be guarding it against the forces of the night that might want to commandeer it before he had a chance to understand the mysteries of Hopkins House.

On the sofa, propping his legs up on the ancient coffee table, Aaron opened the album, and in the very descript, almost calligraphy-like, hand written pages, he began to read the history of the ill-fated Hopkins family and how evil had taken up residence in the brownstone mansion on Farragut Street. The story was detailed and precise, and in order to understand what followed in this most unusual mystery, I will herewith detail the specifics of what Aaron read; although, I will not go into some of the superficial aspects which had no bearing on the case.

Within the pages that follow, I, as a witness of many of the events and confident of others who saw the same, will attempt to lay bare the details of the sordid happenings that have plagued the Hopkins family and led to an unnatural presence in the mansion on Farragut Street.

Part 1: In order to understand how the evil was perpetrated, one must go back to the purchase of a jewellery box by Candace Hopkins in 1906. One day, while window shopping, she found an obscure curio shop near Castro Street. Upon entering the shop, she felt uneasiness when she was greeted by someone whom she assumed was the shopkeeper, an ancient-looking woman with scraggly hair and yellowish, crooked teeth. For some reason, she took Candace by the hand and said, "I know you. You are a member of the Hopkins family."

Perplexed at how the woman could know her, Candace started to leave, but then the old woman said, "Do not leave my child, for I have a magnificent item that is very cheap, and is ideal for a family headed by a man who likes to abuse workers in order to accumulate wealth."

She picked up an old, small jewellery box that measured six by six by six. She stood before Candace smiling, her lower lip almost quivering. "Be aware that when you open the box, for which I have no key, within this box, is a locket that can also be opened. Open this locket at your own peril, because those who are part of the ruling class that makes their God callous greed and avariciousness will suffer dire circumstances, if the locket is opened to reveal what is beneath the cameo that graces the front. If it is not opened, it will guard you from harm in this world and the world to come. It is yours for the princely sum of $1.00, and it will be an investment that assures you of the utmost happiness in a world that measures good fortune in dollars and cents. I offer it to you for protection against the evil of those who acquire wealth on the backs of the poor. You need it child, for you are part of a family that permeates with evil."

Candace, mesmerized by the old woman, reached in her purse, pulled out a dollar, and was handed the box in return. As Candace looked down at her purse, placing the box within, she momentarily looked away from the woman. When she looked up, the woman was gone.

Part 2: When returning home, Candace was careful to tell no one about the box. She planned to get a locksmith to open it the following day. Unfortunately, the 1906 earthquake hit shortly after the purchase of the box. Having escaped from the building during the quake, when the family was safely outside, Candace scurried back into the rubble to recover the box. This risky act incurred the wrath of her father. Harry Hopkins actually slapped his daughter and berated her for risking her life for a silly old box. From that moment on, Candace and her father's relationship was never the same. An intense hatred toward her father grew within Candace, and she became sullen and withdrawn as the family left for Sacramento and returned by train to Manhattan.

Part 3: Within three days of returning home, Candace took the box to a locksmith, who promptly opened it. Seeing the beautiful cameo locket that was inside, Candace placed it around her neck, carefully caressing it, almost as if it had life. She discarded the box in a trash can, and proceeded home.

Once home, her two sisters and mother were admiring the locket when Charlene asked if she could open it to see what was inside. Candace insisted that no one should ever open it, for it was a secret that she must keep. Charlene and her mother, accepted Candace's pleas without hesitation, and it appeared that her younger sister also did, but within the mind of the baby sister was born a genuine need to seek out the locket, and see what was so mysterious about what was inside. This younger sister for years harboured thoughts of opening the locket, but by the time she was 20, she still had not had the opportunity to find the locket without her sister's presence, for Candace never let it *out of her sight.*

Part 4: In 1911, Candace married a young man named Harold Ridgeway, who worked for her father. In fact, it was her father who arranged the marriage. Candace found Harold a slovenly, ill-mannered, arrogant man whom she loathed, but it was her father who insisted she marry him, so that he could have a son to pass the business on to when he died. Although hating him intensely, Candace and he moved into the mansion on Farragut and took the entire third floor for their home. However, it was at this time that the evil began in earnest.

One day, Candace left the locket on her bedroom dresser when she went to work with her father and Harold, so that she could do some downtown shopping and return with them later in the evening. The younger sister noticed when they left that the locket was not being worn by Candace. For so many years she had waited for this opportunity, but she still had to figure out how to go into the third floor bedroom without Charlene and her mother finding out.

Luck would have it that Charlene had become ill, and her mother decided to walk with her to the doctor, leaving the youngest sister alone at home. Now, the stage was set for the youngest sister to finally see what was inside the locket.

As she climbed the stairs to the third floor, she kept looking back for Candace, fearful that she might notice that she did not have the locket, and being so attached to it that she never let it out of her sight, would run home in a panic to retrieve it. Ascending upward, the old wooden stairs seemed to creak especially loud as she walked ever so gingerly, almost as if she was afraid someone or something was in the house with her. Her breathing became so heavy that her large, orb-like breasts seemed to almost tear through the thin fabric of her silk blouse as she ascended, edging slowly but methodically toward her ultimate goal.

As she stepped onto the large third floor landing, her long skirt seemed to be clinging to her generous curves as she was sweating profusely through her tight garments. There was no turning back now.

The bedroom was dark except for a small beam of light that shone through the partially opened curtains and appeared to dance on the dresser, making the locket almost glow. She was finally going to see what was so important that it must never be revealed.

Placing her right hand on the cameo, she rubbed it as she picked it up with her left hand. With some trepidation she prepared to open it, but then put it down.

Looking out the partially drawn curtains, she saw the sun suddenly go behind a cloud and the room became dark, almost as dark as night. She felt as if she was being surrounded by darkness. The room took on a surreal feeling. It was as if it were alive. The walls seemed to vibrate; the ceiling began to creak, the lighting fixture in the middle of the room swayed back and forth.

Confused and bewildered, she started to leave the room, to leave that which she had sought for so long. The door slammed shut. She stood there terrified, not knowing what her next move would be. By trying to open the locket, had she awakened the forces of darkness in what would be a disastrous calamity, or was someone or something telling her to open it, not to leave before her task was completed?

She again reached down for the locket. Picking it up in her right hand, she transferred it to her left hand, cupping it almost as if it were a fragile object that must be protected from harm. Her right thumb and forefinger moved to the clasp. Prying it open slowly, she could hear her laboured breathing as she pulled open that which she had longed to see. When it was half opened, she began to loose her fears, because it appeared to be empty. Smiling, she quickly opened it all the way.

Suddenly, a mist came out of the locket and grew larger and larger, almost taking on the form of a human. She closed the locket, placed it in her sweater pocket and gasped for air.

The mist moved toward the wall, dissipating as it entered it, leaving behind a wet stain on the wallpaper. The evil had been unleashed. She had not merely opened a locket; she had opened the doors of hell, as a demon was now at play in the walls of Hopkins House.

CHAPTER 6
OF MORTAL FORM

Aaron could not help but chuckle at the stories in the album. Evil residing in the walls of a home was about as ridiculous as believing Republicans cared about the working men and women of America. It was so outlandish that he vowed that he had read enough. He closed the album, got up and walked to the bathroom. Looking in the mirror as he washed the dust from the album off his hands, he turned his head to the right and looked at the album on the coffee table. He knew he had closed it, but it had been opened again. He strolled back to the coffee table and saw the book had been opened to the page where he had stopped reading. Easing onto the sofa, he leaned forward and started to read again.

Part 5: The wet stain on the wall caused much discussion and consternation, but the youngest sister's indiscretions were never discovered. However, the locket had mysteriously disappeared. The youngest sister had forgotten that it was in her sweater pocket, and the sweater hung in the closet for years, undisturbed. As the years went by, Candace and her husband began to argue furiously, as did Harry and his wife. Through all this, the youngest sister seemed unaffected as did Charlene.

One evening, in 1914, when Harold came home from work, he said hello to the family, and went upstairs to take a brief nap with Candace. As the family was gathering for dinner, they heard a violent scream from the third floor. Running up the stairs and opening the bedroom door, they found Candace standing over her husband's body, screaming, "It came out of the wall. It came out of the wall."

After investigation by the police, it was determined that Harold had apparently simply died of a heart attack. However, Candace continued to insist that a mist came out of the wall and seemed to embrace the whole room before Harold collapsed onto the floor.

Afterward, she could remember nothing until she was standing over her husband's body shouting and screaming. Her recounting of strange occurrences fell on death ears, both in her household and at police headquarters, but the youngest sister knew that Candace had, no doubt, experienced something strange in the same room where she had opened the locket.

Part 6: After Harold's death, the evil seemed to multiply as Charlene, in 1920, married a man 10 years her junior, Robert McLeay, and they moved into the third floor, exposing themselves to the evil. Since Harold's death, Candace had continued to live in the home, but had moved downstairs, vowing to never sit foot on the third floor again. Meanwhile, the youngest sister had become a great lover of the wild, frenzied, untamed, hedonistic lifestyle. She was consistently out until the early morning, partying with a variety of men, and rumoured to even be attracted to other women. This lifestyle did not set well with her mother or father, and Candace found it deplorable to be the sister of what she called a brazen hussy. Through it all, the youngest sister just smiled and continued her frivolous ways, completely ignoring the machinations and pleas for her to practice a more acceptable lifestyle.

Part 7: In March of 1923, Candace assumed she was home alone and Robert returned early from work. For years, Candace had eschewed the company of men, but she had secretly harboured an intense interest in Robert who was an immensely handsome man with broad shoulders, deep blue penetrating eyes and a tussled head of hair that made him appear a bit roguish. He came into the foyer, preparing to go upstairs. Candace, even though it was early afternoon, was wearing a transparent negligee. She walked down the long hallway toward Robert and the light from the window in the door penetrated her garment, revealing the dark brown nipples of her breasts, and the coal black pubic hair between her soft white thighs. Robert stood still as she gracefully glided toward him, moving as if in slow motion. Her lips parted slightly and she lifted her chin.

Robert's breathing quickened. Candace stopped just far enough from him so the light still revealed her womanliness. Reaching out with both hands, Robert swept her in his arms, and she tilted her head as their lips meet in a long, passionate kiss.

Taking Robert's right hand, Candace led him down the hallway to her bedroom. Unbeknownst to them, they were not alone. The younger sister had actually slipped in unnoticed earlier in the afternoon, and she had gone into the upstairs study. When she heard the front door open she had left the study and was standing in the upstairs doorway, hidden from the view of the two aroused lovers downstairs. Being a hedonist, she was not appalled at all by their behaviour. Rather, she was intrigued by it and crept down the stairs so that she could listen outside the door as they made passionate love. She became so aroused that she lifted her dress and started masturbating, as she fantasized about what Robert's manhood looked like.

Sighing, licking his lips, and easing back on the sofa, Aaron took a deep breath, and started thinking about Rachael. He had seen no pictures of Candace, but if she was related to Rachael, she, no doubt, was a woman of beauty. Well, maybe not beauty. Rachael was probably a little overweight, and she had a few crow's-feet around her eyes. Even her nose was a bit large for a woman. What Rachael had went beyond beauty. There was an intense sexual component to her looks that seemed to make her exude an air of wantonness and hedonism that was brazen, yet subdued. Just the way she walked was alluring. Watching her breathe was arousing. Looking into her intense brown eyes seemed to stimulate passions deep within and stir excitement.

Aaron looked at his crotch and noticed his pants start to grow slowly around his zipper. He reached down with his left hand to adjust his manhood to ease the pain as he tried to get Rachael out of his mind. Yet, he could not obliterate the image of her standing before him in all her seductive, lascivious glory seeming to beckon him into her arms. He longed to possess her, to feel her warmth and explore every centimetre of her being.

Looking out the open window behind his desk, he heard the fluttering of paper, and looked down to notice a page from the album was slowly turning, making him wonder if the album was beckoning him, urging him to continue to explore the strange occurrences at Hopkins House. Of course, even though there appeared to be no breeze coming through the open window, Aaron reasoned that it was the wind that was causing the page to flutter.

He reached down, and turned to the next page, eager to learn more of the mysteries of Hopkins House.

Part 8: As time passed, Candace and Robert continued their clandestine meetings whenever possible. Many times, when the youngest sister would think they might be rendezvousing, she would hide in the study and slip down to eavesdrop on their frantic lovemaking. Although she had many suitors, she could not stop thinking about what it might be like to make love to Robert. The thought of it began to gnaw at her until she devised a scheme to get her sister out of the house on an afternoon that she knew they had set aside for lovemaking. She arranged for a courier to deliver a message only a few minutes before Robert was due home. The message would certainly get her out of the house, because it stated, "Candace, I am in possession of a certain locket that I know would interest you. I will be in the New Rochelle Train Station today between 2 and 4. Come into the station and take a seat in front of the news counter. Bring $100. I will know you, so do not worry about recognizing me. I look forward to returning something that I know you value."

Watching her sister leave, this wanton creature quickly removed all her clothes and put on a towel that barely covered her large, perfectly cylindrical breasts as she pulled it low enough to expose part of the dark brown areola on her left breast. She then tucked in the right bottom of the towel, so that her generous pubic hair that ran down the upper part of her right thigh was exposed. Moving to the bathroom door, she awaited Robert's arrival. When he could not find Candace, he came up the stairs, and just as he got to the landing, he stopped in his tracks as this lustful, perverse hedonist came out of the bathroom. Smiling at him, she said, "So, are you disappointed that Candace is gone for the afternoon?"

She reached up to the area where the towel was secured and pulled it open. As the towel hit the floor, the intense, sexually charged atmosphere exploded in a frenzy of lips, tongues and hands as the two brazenly mauled at one another. Without a word between them, Robert lifted her and carried her into her second floor bedroom where the passionate lovemaking continued unabated for hours. So enthralled with passion that they lost track of time, they were totally unaware when Candace came home from New Rochelle, and intrigued by the moans of passion, went upstairs and boldly opened the bedroom door. Sitting astride Robert, the sister turned her head and said, "Could you please close the door Candace, unless you want to watch your sister get the fucking of her life."

Closing the door, the incident was never mentioned, and Robert never had a liaison with Candace again, as he concentrated all his infidelity on the younger sister. For several weeks the sisters did not speak, and avoided each other whenever possible. Then, one morning Charlene went down for breakfast. On the way down the stairs she was surprised to see Candace coming up the stairs, as she had made it a point to never venture above the second floor after the death of her husband. She assumed Candace was going to her sister's second floor bedroom.

Part 9: About 20 minutes later, Candace joined Charlene in the kitchen. They talked briefly and Charlene went upstairs. Suddenly, a loud scream was heard and the entire house erupted in turmoil as on the third floor, lying on the carpet in the exact same spot where Candace's husband had died years earlier, was the body of Robert, with a look of terror on his face. The coroner determined the cause of death to be a heart attack. Yet, the younger sister, as did Candace, knew the real cause of death was the evil that lurked in that room, or was the real evil within the family? Was the real evil of a more mortal form?

CHAPTER 7
MASSACRE IN HOPKINS HOUSE

Aaron was a practical man, and he put no credence in ghost stories or tales of demons. If you believed in demons, he assumed that you would believe in God, and as an avowed atheist, he saw no evidence of demons or God. All he saw was evil, but it was not the evil perpetrated by demons, it was the evil of men. The biggest evil he saw was the imposition of a system of greed called capitalism that permanently relegated a large number of people to poverty or a marginal existence, so they could be exploited by the privileged classes that got their wealth on the backs of those they saw as commodities rather than human beings.

He looked at the album, wondering whether he should continue reading or not. For a brief moment, he glanced at the mirror on the wall. He saw a strange, tiny light in the mirror, a light that seemed to bounce off the glass and direct itself to the album on the coffee table. The light danced about, and he saw speckles of white dust flutter inside the light. He reached out with his hand and flicked the dusty particles away, but he felt a strange sensation, almost as if his hand was being shocked by tiny electrodes. He looked at his palms and they were sweating. He glanced back at the mirror and the light was gone.

Exhausted and confused, Aaron reclined on the sofa, drifted off to sleep and began to dream. He saw a kaleidoscope of colours that gradually disappeared into a hue of blue that seemed to open up into a black and white vision of his father sitting at the dinner table with a drink in his left hand. As the eleven year old Aaron made his way to the table, his father reached out with his rough, calloused right hand and placed it on his shoulder. He pulled him to his breast, embraced him tightly, and whispered in his ear, "I know you saw me in the garage. What I was doing should be our secret, son. Remember, I love you and your mother very much."

Aaron's love for his father was often difficult, as he knew that he disappointed his dad in many ways. Aaron's interests were much different than his father's, who was a man obsessed with perfection in everything he did. Meantime, Aaron, as a boy and man, saw the work ethic as just an excuse for the wealthy to force the poor to toil for them with the hopes they would some day obtain the same status as the wealthy. He could not help but scoff at how politicians talked about the American work ethic like it was some kind of panacea that would free the working man from the bondage of living from one pay check to the next. He thought it ironic that those who talked the most about the work ethic were the privileged of America who would not last a day in the typical factory where the working class toiled for table scraps while the rich dined on filet mignon and caviar.

He blinked his eyes and almost awakened, before he slowly closed them and fell into another half-asleep, half-awake slumber. Visions of Rachael Hopkins flashed before him, as he imagined what she must look like naked. He envisioned her without clothes and sensed she was a large woman, but well proportioned. He knew that she would excite and arouse the passions of a man like him, who preferred women with some meat on their bones to the painfully skinny women who were the norm for a society that put a premium on beauty. Real beauty, thought Aaron, was a generously proportioned woman with curves that accentuated her womanliness. And, he imagined her with generous pubic hair, rather than the shaved bodies of women that made them look like plucked chickens.

Suddenly awakening, he sat up on the sofa, looked at the album, and knew that he must continue to read about the mysterious occurrences at Hopkins House. It was all just fantasy. Yet, he found himself strangely interested in finding out more about this family, so that he might better understand Rachael Hopkins, and, perhaps, help her put together the pieces of a puzzle that would free her from what she perceived as evil.

Part 10: Three years passed and in 1923, Candace was 44 years old and considered a spinster. Charlene was 41, and had never remarried after the death of Robert. The younger sister was in her thirties and still single, as she preferred the company of a variety of men. To me more exact, she often kept company with two or three men at the same time, which created somewhat of a scandal, and, no doubt, was a source of considerable acrimony between the younger sister and her mother and father. Anna and Harry Hopkins even threatened to disinherit her and turn her out on the streets several times, only to be told that she had plenty of men who would welcome her into their homes. The father, who had become almost unbearable in his arrogance and personal hygiene habits, seemed to relish belittling his daughters and letting his wife know that he had younger women that made a 68 year old man feel young again. Anna Hopkins was stoic and frankly delighted that she did not have to serve the sexual needs of a husband she had grown to deplore.

Part 11: One day, the youngest sister was preparing a box of old clothes for the Salvation Army. She carefully folded and packed many items in an old box, including the sweater containing the locket that had hung in the closet for a decade. She noticed the slight bulge in the pocket as she put the sweater on the top of the pile, suddenly remembering that she had put the locket there many years ago. Just as she was about to retrieve the long lost locket, Charlene knocked on her door. Not wanting Charlene to discover she had the locket, she left it in the pocket, thinking she would retrieve it later. Charlene requested that she come to the kitchen, where Candace had cut her hand and was bleeding profusely. The two of them realized that stitches were necessary, so they took her to the hospital. While they were gone, the Salvation Army pick-up service came by, and Anna Hopkins, not knowing where her daughters were, went to all the rooms gathering the materials that had been packed, including the sweater with the locket in it. The pick-up man left with the sweater and the locket.

Aaron stopped reading, looked up at the old picture hanging on the wall of him and his army buddies and thought about how much significance Rachael put in that silly locket. Yet, as he looked at his comrades-in-arms, he realized just how significant the insignificant can be. He hated the Vietnam War as did his buddies. All they wanted was to survive. Beating the enemy was not ever their consideration. In fact, they had more respect for the enemy than for their superiors back at headquarters and the Pentagon. Their enemies were noble men who were dedicated to a cause; whereas, Aaron and his buddies were all just draftees sent by the politicians in Washington to die for an utterly asinine and ridiculous cause – the cause of promulgating capitalism in a country where capitalism was nothing more than a continuation of the colonial slavery it had suffered through for hundreds of years. They all felt insignificant in the scheme of things, as they were forced to fight an immoral war while the children of the rich and privileged avoided service by hiding in the National Guard or getting cushiony military jobs stateside. Yes, they all felt insignificant, but yet, together, they were all significant, because they were one. They were dedicated to protecting each other, so that they could all return home and put the lunacy of Vietnam behind them. So, he began to understand Rachael's desire to find that locket. She genuinely felt that the insignificant was significant to her relatives. By finding that long lost item, she felt she could make them whole again. By returning that which she conceived as the item that started the evil, she could feel that she had done her part to put the ghosts of the past to rest. He and some comrades-in-arms returned home alive, and they felt that they had made each other whole again. Yet, the past would not die. When they saw Americans waving the flag and singing *God Bless America*, they all sensed that the country was being propagandized into an arrogant self-righteousness that would some day turn the reins of power over to a despot who would again lead young men to their deaths in an immoral and illegal war. Yet, they had all survived and would do all they could to alert others to the follies of arrogance and self righteousness. So, he understood Rachael's quest.

The locket, for Rachael, was the key to ending what she saw as the evil machinations that permeated Hopkins House. Yet, Aaron wondered what its return would accomplish. How would Rachael use it to circumvent the perceived evil trapped in Hopkins House? It did not matter any longer. Aaron knew that he was so enamoured with Rachael that his only course of action was to locate the locket for her.

Exhausted by reading the album, Aaron eased back on the sofa, propped his feet up and dosed off. As he snoozed, thoughts of his father again played like a kaleidoscope in his mind. He had loved his father so much, but always felt that there was a distance there that he could not bridge. There was always that part of his father that seemed to cry out for love and affection. Yet, when he received it from so many people, it was never enough. There was something deep inside his father crying out for understanding, but no one could ever reach the inner most needs of a complicated, distant man who was loved by so many, but understood by none.

Aaron remembered the day he received his draft notice. His father had told him that to serve was lunacy. Why fight in an utterly stupid war for a pack of politicians whose own children would be allowed to avoid service or get some easy stateside duty while the poor and underprivileged died in a foreign land for no reason? After all, his father had influence with the draft board, and he could arrange for his name to be overlooked or for him to get a deferment through other nefarious means. His father was not a politician, but many politicians were beholding to him. In fact, he shared many paramours with these men who liked to project a virtuous image to a public too stupid to see that virtue was preached by the few to the many, while the few laughed at the gullibility of those they ruled. His father always saw through this hypocrisy, and pointed it out to Aaron. His father had taught him many valuable lessons about the fallibility of those who professed virtuousness but lived lives of hideous hypocrisy.

Aaron recalled his childhood which was often traumatic, as he struggled with what he considered neglect from a father obsessed with building wealth. While his mother was loving and kind, she was frequently forced to choose between what she felt was her duty as a wife and her duty as a mother. Through it all, Aaron's grandmother was his salvation, and always was there when Aaron's spirits had sunk so low that he felt there was no way up. He recalled watching her unconscious in the hospital, and how he spent night after night by her bedside, and would beg her to please not die, to please not leave him, because he needed her so much, even at the age of 22. He genuinely felt that her love for him was so powerful that she might actually cheat death to not leave him alone. Yet, death was not to be denied. It was the greatest blow in Aaron's life, to lose someone who had been the guiding light of his life.

Many times after her death, Aaron's melancholy thoughts would overwhelm him. Yet, he seemed to somehow feel her presence, often. As Aaron's mind slipped into that state of sleep that seems to beckon us to let go, to just float into a state of suspended animation, he visualized his grandmother, just as she had been in her 60's. He saw her image moving from a grassy hillside down an old dirt road with the same benign countenance that had defined her as a person who offered solace to the weak and weary. She was smiling with an old, worn hickory stick dangling from the side of her mouth and just a dab of snuff on her lower lip. Her lips started to move, but rather than words, he heard music borne on the hot summer air as she seemed to glow with an essence of peace and tranquility.

He suddenly awakened, but he could still hear the music as if it were all around him. The air became light and he watched the dust particles dance in front of the office lights. He sat on the edge of the sofa, looking about the room. This was not an illusion; there was music in the room, sweet, relaxing, soothing music. As he looked down at the album, the harmony became more sullen and steady until it paused and there was silence.

The silence became deafening. It seemed to penetrate the room and the quietness actually made Aaron cup his hands and place them over his ears. Breathing heavily, he continued to stare at the album. He saw the words *Part 12,* and knew that he was no longer going to dismiss this whole affair as superstitious claptrap.

Part 12: In 1925, the family had settled into a steady diet of hatred for one another as animosities grew to the point that most of them were living in their own rooms with little intermingling. What was long ago a happy, harmonious, loving household had grown into a cacophony of sullenness, harshness and malevolence since the younger sister had unleashed the horror in Candace's room many years before. Late in October, when the youngest sister came home one evening from a night of debauchery; she removed her clothes as she was going up the stairs, discarding them along the way. Completely naked, she entered her room and lay on the bed with her legs spread, looking in the mirror on the wall near the foot of the bed. She admired her dark, long, curly pubic hair as it glistened in the moonlight that fluttered through the slightly drawn drapes. She began to gently massage her mound of desire and reflect on the evening that had included unbridled sexual adventures with two virile men who made her feel like a wanton hussy of the night. But, she felt no shame. Why should she feel shame she thought. What was more shameful, her wantonness or the shame of those who pointed the finger of condemnation in a society of hypocrites. She only felt exhilaration and joy in knowing that she was a woman who revelled in the realization of all the possibilities offered for pleasure.

She would soon find out that this was a night that would not end with exhilaration, but with death and a permanent stigma on Hopkins House. The final evil machinations that would destroy this family and many others were fermenting in a bedroom on the third floor. The end was at hand, and it would be of the most diabolical sort.

Part 13: As the younger sister reflected back on the evening, she heard someone climbing the stairs. Not wanting to interrupt her thoughts of the pleasure she had experienced earlier, she continued her self-exploration, assuming that it was her sister, Charlene, going up to her third floor room. Little did she know that Charlene was already up there, and the person climbing the stairs was Candace, who had consistently avoided the room after her husband, Harold, had died in it. However, the younger sister would eventually find out that Candace had been in there one other time, one other deadly time.

At this point, I must digress a bit and return to the death of Harold, which was deemed an accident by the police. Harold met his death when Candace was in the room, but it was fear that killed him, not just a heart attack. The impetus for the fear was a manifestation of evil called up by Candace. Candace entered the room and looked at Harold. She told him that she was tired of arguing and that she wished him dead, so that she would no longer look upon his sullen face. At that moment, Harold started to laugh and insisted that he would never leave her until her parents were dead and he had his share of the Hopkins' fortune. Candace turned, walked over to the spot on the wall and whispered something that was indiscernible to Harold. She then proceeded to sit in a nearby chair and watched as Harold fought for a breath that would not come. She laughed and then screamed in terror, or was it a scream of happiness?

The second time Candace was in the room was when Robert was killed. Although it was assumed Candace never went into the room after the death of her husband, she did enter it on the day Charlene passed her on the stairs to confront Robert about his trysts with her younger sister. As he stood before her, telling her that she was no longer of any interest to him, she turned, walked to the wall and whispered something that was indiscernible to Robert. Suddenly, he grasped at his heart and fell to the floor as Candace left and went downstairs.

What follows is not for the faint of heart, because herein, I am going to describe heinous, brutal acts of murder that brought the evil to its apex. I describe them not to shock, but to lay bare the true horror that abounds in Hopkins House.

As the younger sister lay on the bed, gently rubbing her genitals, she heard a rustling sound upstairs, then a loud thud. She arose, put on her robe, peeked out her door and up the stairs. There was silence. Then, she saw Candace suddenly appear at the doorway with a sinister look on her face, as she looked down the stairs at her younger sister.

Curious, the younger sister ascended the stairs to see what was going on. As she reached the top stair, Candace came out onto the landing, grabbed her by the hand and led her toward the room. Candace manoeuvred her way to the rear and just as they got to the door, she violently shoved her unsuspecting sister onto the floor. Lying on the floor was Charlene, who had been bound and gagged. Candace slapped the younger sister across the face and straddled her. As her sister struggled for breath, Candace turned her over on her stomach and grabbed the rope that was on the bed. Just as the sister tried to arise and regain her composure, Candace kicked her in the groin. Placing her foot on the back of her head, Candace tied her arms and gave her a vicious kick in the small of the back. Barely conscious, the sister offered no resistance as she whimpered in pain.

Candace, breathing heavily, sat in a chair near the bed and looked at the infamous spot on the wall. She seemed to slip off into a trance, alternately closing and opening her eyes. She looked at her two sisters and a sinister smile crept across her mouth. She got up, walked across the room, actually stepping on Charlene's chest, and laughed out loud as she heard bones break. She slowly moved toward the far wall, bent over, placing her ear to the spot. For a few seconds she seemed to listen to something. Then, she turned and walked out the door.

Candace calmly walked down the stairs and out to the storage shed behind the house where she picked up an axe, a hatchet and a hammer. She walked back into the kitchen, removed three large butcher knives from a drawer and went upstairs, placing all the items on the bed. The two sisters looked in horror at Candace, but were even more horrified when she sat down on the bed and smiled at them. She again peered toward the wall, and with deep breaths seemed to develop an aura invincibility.

The three sisters heard the front door downstairs as it opened and their mother called out to ask if anyone was home. Candace put her right index finger to her lips indicating that her sisters should be quiet. To drive home the point, she also placed her left hand on the hatchet. She picked up the hatchet and moved toward the door; calling out to her mother to come up to the third floor as she and her sisters had something important to show her.

Surprised to hear Candace from the third floor, Anna Hopkins rapidly ascended the stairs. As she approached the bedroom door, Candace was standing in the doorway smiling, the hatchet hidden in her left hand behind her back. She stepped into the hallway, motioning with her right hand for her mother to enter. As Anna looked into the room, she gasped in disbelief as she saw two of her daughters bound on the floor. Meanwhile, Candace shifted the hatched from her left hand to her right, and just as her mother turned to ask what was going on, she used the blunt end of the hatchet to strike her mother across the forehead. The skin broke slightly but no blood came out as Anna Hopkins crumbled to the floor unconscious.

Candace smiled. Then, she looked at her two sisters and winked. Viciously kicking her mother in the side, she turned her over with her right foot by placing it under her stomach and lifting upward. She tied her hands, gagged her and sat down on the chair, staring at the spot on the wall.

Waiting for her father to come home, Candace told her younger sister that all this was her fault. That it was she who had unleashed the evil, because she knew it was she who had opened the locket. If it had not been for that, the tranquility that abounded in the family would have continued, but that she alone bore the burdens of what was about to happen. She was the one responsible for all that was about to occur, and that she would witness the evil that she had unleashed.

As Anna Hopkins regained consciousness and the two bound sisters struggled to loosen their bonds, they heard the downstairs door open, and knew that their only chance for survival was the father they had all grown to hate. Candace went to the bed, picked up the hatchet and moved toward the door, where she called out to her father and said that they were all in the third floor bedroom and they had something they needed to show him. Again, she waited for her next victim by standing in the doorway. As her father moved toward the door, she came into the hallway, hiding the hatchet in her right hand behind her back, letting her father enter the room first. Just as he saw the three women on the floor, he turned to face Candace and was hit with a glancing blow to the left side of his head. Blood gushed out of the wound as he collapsed onto the floor. Still conscious, he struggled to get up, grabbing Candace by the left leg. She brought the hatched down across his shoulder, digging it so deep into flesh and bone that she had to struggle to pull it out. With his left arm useless and bleeding profusely, he tried to grab her left leg with his right hand. She brought the hatchet straight down so hard across his wrist that she severed his hand. She giggled slightly as the hand lay on the floor still twitching, the fingers moving rhythmically as if they were tapping out a tune. No longer capable of struggling, her father fell onto his back. Blood from his wounds filled the brown carpeted floor, seeping underneath Anna as she tired to scream but could not because of the gag in her mouth. Candace walked to the bed and picked up a butcher knife. Sinisterly grinning, she moved toward her mother and removed her gag.

She moved to her two sisters and also removed their gags. She told all three of them that she wanted to hear their screams, because it was a symphony to her ears. Their screams vibrated off the walls as Candace bent over her father with the hatchet and incessantly chopped at his left shoulder until his arm was severed. She picked up the arm and threw it on her mother. She strode over to the bed, almost as in slow motion, picked up the butcher knife, turned and glided back toward her father. Unfortunately, he was partially conscious and his eyes almost popped out of the sockets as Candace lay the knife on the floor in the pool of blood that was forming around her father. She bent over, unbuckled his belt and rather than remove his shoes, she just picked up the hatchet and chopped off his feet at the ankle. Pulling his pants down, she removed his underwear, grabbed his penis by its head and sliced it off with a butcher knife as far down as possible. This final act of barbarity was too much for her father, as he closed his eyes and embraced death with thankfulness.

Holding her father's penis in her right hand and the butcher knife in the left, she walked over to her mother, kicked her father's severed limb from the stomach, bent to her knees and rubbed the penis on her mother's lips. As her mother shook her head in disgust, Candace plunged the knife into her stomach, turning it from side to side in order to maximize the pain. She put the knife in so deep that it became stuck in the floor. Anna Hopkins was still conscious, as Candace gave up on removing the knife, went to the bed and picked up the axe. She stood over her mother's head grinning from ear to ear. She almost laughed out loud as she swung the axe over her head and brought it down onto Anna's skull, splitting it wide open down the middle. Brains spattered onto the wall and Charlene, as Candace let out a deep, guttural sound that seemed to originate from deep within her soul and reverberate off the walls as her sisters, so filled with terror they could no longer scream, awaited their fate with quiet resignation and only slight whimpering.

Candace lifted the axe from her mother's skull, wiped some blood off her forehead with her left hand, and walked over to Charlene. Looking to her left, she noticed her youngest sister squirming frantically trying to crawl toward the door. She moved diagonally to cut off her sister's path, looked down at her and told her she would be privileged to watch the end of the carnage, but first she would see to it that she was unable to crawl any further. She reversed the axe, and used the blunt end to crush her sister's knees. The screams in reaction to the excruciating pain were actually music to Candace's ears. The delight she was taking in the carnage made the fear even more pronounced as her two sisters awaited their fate.

Moving toward Charlene, Candace kneeled next to her whimpering sister, leaned on the axe handle as she stood the blade on the floor and pointed to the spot on the wall. Through smiling lips she uttered to her sister, "That is what you can thank your beloved younger sister for, Charlene. It is she who slipped into my room and opened the locket. It is she who caused all the family pain. It is she who made me unleash the evil in this room that killed my husband and yours. I am but the humble instrument of the demon she unleashed. Her act tore this family asunder, and I will see that for all eternity, we are all locked in the embrace of the evil she has unleashed through her unmitigated act of betrayal. The locket is lost forever, and so are all of us."

She stood above Charlene, untied her hands, but was careful to step on her outstretched arms as she straddled her body, holding the axe slightly above Charlene's chest. She smiled and heaved the axe above her head, bringing it down swiftly, cutting Charlene's right arm of at the elbow. Laughing out loud, she raised it again and brought it down on her left arm, cutting it off at the shoulder. Still conscious, Charlene looked at her sister, not saying a word. Yet, her eyes seemed to beg for release from the hell she was enduring. However, Candace was not through with the tortuous misery she was inflicting.

The younger sister valiantly managed to turn over. She struggled to crawl toward Charlene, her battered knees causing excruciating pain. Just as she reached Charlene, Candace meandered leisurely over to the wall and put her ear next to the spot.

Charlene mumbled like a sobbing child as her younger sister struggled to sit up, reached down and pulled Charlene into her arms, cradling her like a baby. Both sisters begged for death to end their suffering as Candace walked over, axe by her side, and brought the flat end down hard onto Charlene's right knee. As Charlene screamed, Candace swivelled the axe and brought down the sharp edge hard onto Charlene's right leg, cutting it off slightly above the knee. Laughing, she walked to the bed, picked up one of the knives and crossed in front of her sisters to the wall. Dropping to her knees, she put the knife handle onto the floor and pointed the forty centimetre blade toward her stomach. She looked at her dying sisters and said, "You live to see me die, if you can somehow crawl to the front door down three flights of stairs, perhaps you may escape the terror of Hopkins House. I die, knowing that you will both join me after death, forever locked in the embrace of the demon that now makes us all captives of the evil in Hopkins House."

Candace leaned forward, plunging the knife deep into her chest. The wound made a hollow, sucking sound and she collapsed onto the blade, suspended in air, a smile still on her face. A mist seemed to lift from her body and move toward the wall behind her, then disappearing.

As the two sisters watched in horror, Charlene looked up at her now, obviously loving sister, and realized that there was no hope for her. She whispered that she loved her and that she should leave her and crawl down the three flights of stairs to safety and rescue. The younger sister, crying and sobbing, shook her head and said she would not leave her. Charlene smiled and died in her arms.

Three flights of stairs were an incredible obstacle to someone with battered knees who could barely move, but she managed to reach the door and then crawled to the landing above the stairs. Looking down the three flights of stairs, she knew that it was impossible for her to get down them to the front door. She would die there in misery, waiting for rescue from someone who would never come, and even if they did, they could not hear her through the thick, oak front door. Her only hope was to crawl back to the bedroom of horrors and open a window, so she could scream out, and hope that someone in the back alley behind the mansion would hear her. As she rotated her body 180 degrees, she saw that the bedroom door had been closed, but by whom or what? As she managed to reach up and turn the doorknob, it did not move. It had been locked. She was now stranded in the hallway, with no access to the one room with a back alley window. There was no hope. She turned around, crawled back to the landing and managed to lift herself up by grabbing the banister. Looking down the open stairwell at the floor below, she knew what she must do. There was no way she could get down the stairs. Her pain was excruciating, and as she looked at the marble floor below, it seemed to be beckoning to her. Her only relief from the pain was death, and she was the only one capable of releasing herself from the intense misery. She thought of the evil that had been wrought on her family as a result of her curiosity that had apparently unleashed an evil demon in Candace's mind, if not in reality. She felt deeply responsible for all that had occurred. The family had been torn asunder and now she, too, would meet her end alone in Hopkins House, where evil was a permanent resident that had taken up lodging when they returned from San Francisco. She wondered why Candace had not slain her like the rest of the family. She noticed the door to the inner study was open. She crawled to the room, reached up to the desk, and pulled down a pencil and a note pad. She wrote down in her own hand all that had transpired and led to the day of evil. After recording the events, she crawled back to the landing, pulled herself up, leaned over the banister, breathed heavily, closed her eyes, tilted her stomach on the top of the railing, leaned over and plunged to the marble floor below, ending her suffering, but beginning another chapter in the history of evil in Hopkins House.

Aaron closed the album, leaned back on the sofa and propped his feet on the coffee table. Rubbing his chin with his left hand, he reflected on what he had read. This would be a case like none he had ever encountered before in his storied career. Yet, Rachael Hopkins was one client whom he would not let down. He was committed now. He was determined, to not only find the locket, in spite of the fact he believed the idea of evil emanating from a piece of jewellery was asinine, but to find out what was really behind the massacre in Hopkins House.

CHAPTER 8
SOMETHING COLD & CLAMMY IN THE DARKNESS

Having spent a restless night trying to sleep, but being constantly awakened by visual imagines of the massacre he had read about, Aaron was dozing off on the sofa when at 4:00 PM a messenger delivered a message with a request from Rachael asking Aaron to arrive promptly at dusk to discuss his reactions to the album musings about Hopkins House.

The sun was just going down when Aaron knocked on the huge oak door at Hopkins House, but the pounding was obviously falling on death ears, so he pulled the bell three times. After a couple of minutes, he gave up, and as the sun disappeared behind the horizon, he walked down the steps, but suddenly heard the door open behind him. Turning around, he saw Rachael, standing in the doorway smiling at him. The white silk dress she was wearing was made of incredibly thin material, and it was obvious she had not bothered to put on a bra or panties. Her dark, coal black hair flowed gently over her shoulders. The erect nipples of her breasts came to points like two huge mountain peaks jutting high into the sky. The dress was low cut enough to expose the upper half of her breasts, and the huge orbs seemed to be fighting to free themselves from the imprisonment of material that was obviously fighting a losing battle to keep them from being exposed.

As Aaron's gaze moved downward, the streetlamp seemed to cast a direct glow on Rachael's lower extremities, as the dress formed indentations around her mound of desire. That was when Aaron knew she was not wearing panties as the darkness of her black pubic hair actually showed through the dress. He began to feel pain as his manhood became erect in his briefs and protruded toward the top of his pants.

"Well, Mr. Adams, are you going to just stand there and look at me all night, or are you coming in?"

"I may have to think about that. Right now, looking at you all night is a viable option, one which would certainly be pleasurable."

"You know how to make a woman blush, Aaron. Why don't you come in, and you can get a closer look at me." Rachael said as she turned and gave Aaron an incredible view of a curvaceous butt that, like the rest of her body, seemed to cry for attention from an attentive lover.

Aaron bolted up the stoop like a teenager on his first date, taking two steps at a time. He got up them so fast he almost bumped into Rachael in the doorway.

Taking Rachael's left arm, he escorted her down the hall, and into the sitting room. They eased onto the sofa, and Rachael said, "I had some liquor and food delivered last night, Aaron. May I offer you some scotch, and perhaps a bite to eat?"

"That sounds delightful. I hope you will join me."

"I am afraid that eating and drinking will put more weight on my already somewhat generous body, but I will gladly get my nourishment by watching you eat." Said Rachael as she got up and sensuously meandered out of the room and into the kitchen.

Aaron looked around the room, and again, as he had done on his first visit, noticed that Rachael was obviously not an accomplished housekeeper. The dust was very thick on the tables and the curtains looked like they had not been cleaned in decades. There was mustiness to the room that almost made breathing difficult, or was it the thought of the magnificent sexiness of Rachael that was causing Aaron's laboured breathing. Aaron shifted his weight slightly, and felt something under the sofa cushion. He reached down and pulled out an old 3 by 5 picture frame that had been lodged between the armrest and the cushion.

It was a black and white photo of an obviously teenage Rachael, but she was in period costume for some reason. As Rachael entered the room, she smiled as she placed the silver tray on the table in front of Aaron.

"That was taken one Halloween when I dressed as a turn of the century matron. I was a cute little thing wasn't I? I am afraid that my father insisted that I dress as a lady. He had no use for the more frivolous Halloween costumes. I always wanted to be a witch or a demon of some type, but he would not hear of it. I am afraid he was a very forceful man, who made all of us fearful of displeasing him for many years, until we reached a more rebellious stage."

"Well, I can certainly relate to that. My own father was a pretty forceful man, too. However, I was never very rebellious as a youth. I saved it for adulthood. My big rebellious stage actually started when I was in the army and saw how authority was used to subjugate people. I found out that thinking people was what our government feared most. I am afraid that my military superiors were actually happy when my tour of duty ended."

Rachael sat so close to Aaron that, as she crossed her legs, she touched him with the toe of her shoe. Not making a move to stop the contact, she just smiled and leaned back on the sofa, exposing her leg about thirty centimetres above the knee. The sexual tension between the two was so thick it could almost be cut by a knife.

Aaron leaned forward slightly and placed his hand on Rachael's exposed knee. He glided it gently up to the hem of her dress. She licked her lips and tilted her head, inviting a kiss. Their lips met. A torrent of passion poured out as they embraced and they explored the warmth of each others mouths, their tongues darting about like serpents squiggling across a hot path on a blustery, steamy, hot, humid summer day.

Rachael wiggled out of Aaron's arms and said with a raspy voice as she longingly gazed at him, "Aaron, you have no idea how long it has been since I have been filled with a man and experienced the exquisite rapture of what it is like to be a woman. The thought of being made love to, especially by you is almost overwhelming. I may live in a Victorian home with Victorian furniture, but I am far from having a Victorian attitude about sex."

"Rachael," Aaron whispered as he took her in his arms again and pulled her closer. "You are a sexual Goddess. I have never been so enamoured with a woman in all my life. I have fought to hide my erections since the first minute I laid eyes on you."

Giggling, Rachael replied, "You did not do a very good job of hiding your erections. Believe me; the size of the bulge in your pants caught my eye more than once."

Aaron gave her the grin with all the front teeth showing. "Are you ready to do something about it?"

Standing up, Rachael looked into Aaron's eyes. "I hope you are not disappointed. I am not a perfectly proportioned woman. I do have my bulges and sags."

"You bulge and sag in all the right places," Aaron said as he stood up and began to unbuckle his belt.

Rachael reached down and removed her tight laced Victorian high heels as she balanced herself on the sofa arm, first with her right hand and then her left. While she was doing this Aaron had unzipped his pants and removed them and his shoes. He took off his coat, tie and shirt and stood there in his briefs.

As Aaron breathed heavily, Rachael reached down to her dress hem and slowly pulled it up toward her breasts. Just as Aaron had suspected, she had no panties on as her coal black pubic hair that reached almost up to her navel and expanded right and left onto her thick, soft thighs glistened with beads of perspiration while Aaron gazed hungrily at the extremely wide opening that exposed her vulva that looked like it was pulsating rhythmically in anticipation of what was about to occur. Aaron had grown tired of the numerous women who shaved their pubic area. Finally, he was looking at a real woman, a woman who was not afraid to be naturally beautiful.

As she slowly pulled the dress above her breasts, Aaron concentrated on the stomach that was somewhat full, but not fat. The slight bulge was actually sexy as he fantasized about what it was going to feel like to grab it with his hands as she stood up against the wall while he ploughed deep within her from behind. Looking at her huge navel, he imagined what it would be like to pull out of her and deposit his man batter in it.

As she lifted the dress over her head, he noticed that she did not shave under her arms. The thick black hair had probably never seen a razor, so she was also Victorian in that respect or she had just not fallen victim to the crass commercialization of the razor companies that introduced the idea of shaving as being sexier.

"You are beautiful," whispered Aaron, as he took her in his arms, holding her like a fragile piece of porcelain.

Rachael shivered with anticipation as Aaron's hands began to roam casually over her body, working their way to the cheeks of her shapely, generous ass. As his hands wandered to her front, gradually working their way through the patch of thick hair between her legs, she moaned with pleasure as Aaron slid two fingers into her chamber of desire. His kisses were delicate, passionate and sublime as both their heads began to spin with anticipation of the passion that lay ahead. Sexual energy had bubbled to the surface and there was no holding back now as their mouths locked in a lingering kiss.

Rachael whispered into Aaron's ear as she removed his briefs, "Fill me Aaron, fill me with the exquisite girth of this magnificent specimen of manhood."

She grabbed his member with her right hand, rubbing it gently, but determinedly. They gently eased to the floor and she felt him glide deep within her gapping opening. She whispered to him, "I need for you to taste me."

Obligingly, Aaron lifted himself and methodically worked his way toward the root of her passion, gently gliding over her breasts, taking time to fondle them, kissing the surface and soothingly blowing on her nipples as she sighed passionately in anticipation of what she so desperately longed to feel. As his face rested on her beautiful but slightly paunchy stomach, Aaron thought back to the Victorian paintings of nude women he had seen in his youth. Having a generous, but shapely stomach and broad hips was always portrayed as a desirable quality in women by the artists of the day. Aaron thought that he was making love to one of the women whom he had often fantasized about in his youth. He worked his way to her navel and began to encounter a dark patch of coarse hair that he followed down to her pubic area where he buried his face in the thick, dark, soft hair that stretched generously across her pelvic area and extended half-way around her front thigh. He was home, and took up residence for what seemed like hours.

After a long interlude between Rachael's legs, Aaron felt her gently push at his shoulders, and he instinctively rolled over on his back. Rachael cuddled up beside him, kissing him long and deep. Then, she crawled on top of him and moved slowly down between his legs, tracing her way with her tongue as if she was following a road map to pleasure. She took his member in her mouth and seemed to worship and adore it, as if it was a God. It seemed as if it had become a life force for her. It was like it was the only thing keeping her alive. If she let go of it, she would die. She was a willing slave to his erection.

Methodically slowing down each time Aaron seemed to be reaching a climax, the frantic adoration of Rachael continued for almost half an hour, until she finally eased up and crawled on top of Aaron, impaling herself on the object of her desire and riding him like a talented jockey guiding a thoroughbred to the finish line. As if victorious, she let out a long, loud moan as they both reached a furious finish to their magnificent, passionate love ride.

As they lay beside each other on the floor, Rachael put her hands behind her head, exposing her hairy underarms. Aaron felt a new rise between his legs as he turned and gently blew on her underarm hair, wrapping his arms around her as he rubbed under her left arm with his right hand. How erotic it was to be with such a natural woman. She was truly a Victorian in many ways, but her wantonness was anything but Victorian. They continued making love for hours until Aaron finally lay exhausted before her as she smiled triumphantly and said, "What's wrong old man, am I too much woman for you?"

Shaking his head and laughing, Aaron was too weak to reply. They cuddled up in each others arms and drifted off to sleep.

They lay wrapped in each others arms on the floor until 12:00 midnight, when Aaron awakened and stared through the darkness at Rachael. She seemed to be barely breathing. He curiously looked for the rise and fall of her chest, but it was intensely dark, so dark that he could barely make out her gorgeously hard orbs that seemed to jute into the air like twin skyscrapers in downtown Manhattan. It was acutely quiet, so quiet you could hear the proverbial pin drop. He listened for the sound of her breathing, but heard nothing. Just as he was about to put his finger under her nose to feel her breath, he heard the floor creaking near the doorway. He turned to his right and stared into the blackness. The blackness was so thick and dark that it seemed to surround him. It was almost as if the blackness was moving toward him, embracing him in darkness.

He felt uneasy as he sat up just staring into the blackness. The room seemed to be alive. He gazed to his left. He turned his head half way to the right and looked behind him. Chills ran up his spine and his breathing became laboured as he continued to move his head from side to side, expecting to see something in the dark, but there was nothing there, just a feeling, nothing more. He lay back down on his back and reached down to hold Rachael's right hand with his left hand. He slightly extended his right hand out from his side with the palm up. He slumbered off and just as he was about to fall into a deep sleep, something touched his right hand, something cold and clammy in the darkness.

CHAPTER 9
HARBINGER OF DESPAIR

Aaron immediately bolted up to a sitting position, awakening Rachael in the process. She turned to him and quizzically said, "What is wrong, Aaron?"

"Something touched me in the dark?"

"Dear Aaron, I have tried to tell you that there are forces at work within this house that are extremely sinister. You have just had an encounter with a ghost."

Smiling and nodding his head, Aaron replied, "Rachael, you may be right, but until I actually see a ghost and converse with it, I think I will remain sceptical. What I cannot see and put my hands on does not exist for me."

Rachael nearly burst out in laughter as she said, "Aaron, if you only knew the truth. The truth is often stranger than fiction. The day will come when you reflect back on this night, and realize that ghosts are as real as you and I are. You felt the touch of one of the sinister inhabitants of Hopkins House. Do not doubt too much, for those who carry their doubting too far are easier prey for the ghosts of Hopkins House. You read the album and know of the Hopkins deaths, but there have been others. Doubters, like you, have inhabited Hopkins House and met untimely ends or suffered from traumatic breakdowns. There is an ancient Japanese myth that says when a particularly violent act that leads to death occurs in a house, the parties involved in that act are trapped in perpetuity within the walls of the home, and as time passes these spirits begin to recent intrusions by the living into their world of darkness that envelopes them like a warm blanket on a cold night. This is such a house, and the spirits here deeply recent intrusions. For that reason, this place harbours evil of the most malevolent and diabolical kind.

"I lend no credence to any tales of ghosts, and I cannot understand how you can live within this sinister place, thinking that you are among ghosts."

"They have already harmed me as much as they can. I do not fear them any longer. I am at peace here, but I must put them to rest. Only by finding that locket will I be able to bring the terrible manifestations of evil here to an end."

"Then, I will do all I can to find that locket, but I must know where it was when it first left this house. I know it was picked up by the Salvation Army, but where was it taken?"

Rachael looked directly in Aaron's eyes, and said, "The original thrift store was on 43rd Street, and the building is still there I am sure, but that is the extent of my knowledge."

"Can you tell me what the sweater looked like?"

"It was a Cashmere Cardigan with an embroidered design of a butterfly over the left breast. It was a size 12, but because of the large breasts of the Hopkins sister who wore the sweater, the butterfly design was extremely stretched out. As you can tell by looking at me, heredity indicates a history of rather large breasts in the Hopkins women."

"Yes, I certainly can say that heredity has been generous to at least one of the Hopkins women," said Aaron as he smiled impishly.

"My breasts and the rest of my body have certainly enjoyed your attention tonight," said Rachael as she got up and began putting on her clothes.

Aaron, taking this as his cue to do the same, began putting on his clothes, as it became obvious that Rachael was not going to ask him to spend the night.

Walking to the front door together, Aaron noticed Rachael look down rather strangely at the marble foyer that was at the foot of the stairwell above. This, he thought, was the very spot where the younger sister had met her demise. Taking Rachael's hand, he looked sympathetically at her, smiled slightly and without saying a word, let her know that he understood the sadness she felt for those who had died so horribly many years ago.

After they kissed goodnight, Rachael said in her low husky voice, "I know you will help me end the misery that dwells here my dearest Aaron."

When the alarm rang at 8:00 A.M., Aaron groggily got out of bed as he had slept very little. All night he had reflected on the wonderful sexual adventure he had experienced with Rachael. His usual morning erection was even worse, but he smiled and thought to himself that he would save it for Rachael as he had definite plans for a repeat of the previous night's escapade.

His first stop was the abandoned thrift store on 43rd Street that was bounded on both sides by pawn shops that catered to those who had to part with valuables and family heirlooms in order to survive in a society that offered no social safety net to the marginalized citizens who struggled for survival. The building was boarded up on the first floor, but he looked at the second floor and saw that there were plants on the fire escape. Obviously, someone was residing there. The double doors into the building were boarded up, so he walked around the block and down the rear alley to the back of the building where dilapidated, rotten looking stairs led to a second floor door.

Knocking for what seemed like minutes, the rotten, partially painted door was finally opened by an old man of about 80, with most of his teeth missing. He was just another example of those who had been relegated to live in poverty by a society that had no heart or compassion.

"Hi, I am looking for someone who might know something about the old thrift store that used to operate downstairs."

The old man, hunched over like Charles Laughton in the 1930's version of *The Hunchback of Notre Dame*, spoke in a low squeaky voice, "Well, I worked there from 1923 until last year when they closed it up, because some of the younger workers tried to form a union. Was there for 60 years, and they just told me goodbye. No pension, no nothing. Just told me I was too old to work in their new place, but I knew the real reason why. They moved up town and think they gotta high class thrift store now, and they don't want no old man hanging around. They said I could stay on in my apartment for $200 a month until they got a buyer. Hell, that is almost half my social security check. They acted like they was doing me a favour, but I know they just wanted me here in hopes people would not break in if they thought someone was living here. Maybe I can help you young man, come on in and have a seat."

Aaron walked into the musky smelling, dingy, old one room apartment and took a seat on a packing crate at a piece of plywood propped up between two rows of cinder blocks that was his kitchen table. Aaron noticed that there were two unopened containers of cat foot on the table, but no cat in sight. He was most likely eating it himself, as he could probably not afford food in a society that cared nothing about the less fortunate. He had spent a life-time struggling for survival, no doubt, and now, as he was preparing to die, he was still told by the world's most callous, uncaring society that he had not been allowed to live with any dignity, and he would not even be afforded any dignity when he was nearing the end of a life that meant nothing to those who lived in avaricious splendour on the backs of people like him. Damn, thought Aaron, while rich, religious assholes live in iron gated communities and sit in their teak wood pews in palatial churches, they never even think about people like this poor, old, worn out man with no hope in a corrupt society based on greed.

Smiling at the old man, Aaron asked, "So, you were here since 1923?"

Easing onto the crate across from Aaron, the old man said, "Yes, I have worked for them almost all my life. I was an alcoholic, and they always let me have a bowl of soup as long as I would listen to a few words about Jesus, and pretend like I was saved. The executives all get a nice salary and a generous retirement plan, but the workers like me don't get nothing, but a pat on the back and told that we will be rewarded in the end for helping them do God's work. Frankly, I coulda used a little reward down here on earth rather than waiting until I get to heaven. I sure look forward to heaven, cause I spent enough time in hell down here."

"Well, I am afraid heaven may only be an invention of the wealthy to keep the poor from rebelling. Frankly, I don't see much religion in this country. I see plenty of preaching and finger-pointing, but real religion is a pretty scarce commodity. Since Ronald Reagan became President, compassion is about as scarce as water in a desert."

The old man laughed loudly, exposing his gums and said, "Now them is good words to live by mister. Damn good words. You are my kind of guy. You got your finger right on the pulse of things in this here country. My name is Joe Spader, and I is 83 years old. Sure wish I had a drink to offer you."

"Well, thank you Joe. I am Aaron Adams, a private investigator, and I am trying to find an object that was sent to the store downstairs back in the 20's."

"Whatta you looking for? I was always around, either drunk or working. Maybe I can help you."

"I am looking for a locket that would have been in a cardigan sweater with a butterfly embroidered on the breast pocket."

"Damn, Mr. Adams, I don't believe it. I remember that like it was yesterday. Damn thing caused an uproar like you wouldn't believe. Had them self-righteous holy rollers praying day and night. They was scared to death. They was convinced the devil had done come a calling. I gotta kick outta watching them hypocrites wiggle and squirm with fear for once cause they was always acting so high and mighty."

Totally surprised that his very first call in regards to the locket had led to pay dirt, Aaron could not believe his good fortune. "Can you relate to me exactly what transpired?"

"Of course I can. Some rich old woman gave the sweater to our pick up man. He brought the whole box of things in and just put them in the sorting room. We peons was a going through the stuff being watched by one of the supervisors to make sure we didn't steal nothing. He never touched nothing usually, just stood there and watched like some high and mighty asshole who thought we was a bunch of heathen losers who were lucky they would give us a bowl of soup for working our asses off 12 hours a day so they could pass out the stuff or sell it, and use the money to build themselves fancy offices and pay themselves big salaries. Of course, I seen many of them walk off with the really nice stuff, but we workers never got nothing but an occasional moth eaten piece of clothing that they wouldn't even put out to sell."

Aaron was really warming to the story, and the old man could see his interest was piqued. He seemed to take delight in knowing that he was giving Aaron something he needed.

"Anyway, I picked up the sweater. It was really beautiful. I noticed the right pocket I believe it was, sagged a bit. I figured there was something in it, but before I could reach in and get it out, the supervisor come a running over, and he grabbed the sweater right outta my hands. I knew what he was up to. He wanted it for himself. He knew the thing was really valuable."

"You could see the greed in his eyes. He knew he had hold of a real piece of valuable merchandise. Then, when he noticed the pocket sagging, he really got bug eyed. He must have thought he was really going to make a haul. Anyway, he reached in and took out this locket that was inside the pocket. He took one look at it, and he screamed, shouted something about the devil had come a calling, dropped the sweater and locket, told me to pick it up and get rid of it."

Aaron could not believe his luck. He had never had a case where his very first call in search of answers had yielded such a treasure trove of information. Looking with amazement at Joe, Aaron said, "And what did you do with it?"

"Well, I took the sweater and sold it. Have to say, I wound up with enough to buy me two really high quality bottles of scotch. Then I was a little worried about the locket. They was something strange about it. It looked like one of them things. What do you call um? Yeah, it was kinda like a cameo. Only thing was, it felt really warm, almost hot. In the center was a weird looking white raised piece of what looked like ivory I suppose since I don't think they had plastic in them days. The cameo looked kinda like a Halloween devil mask, and at the top on each side was the number 6. Then at the bottom right under the mask-like thing was another 6. That was it 666. I guess that is what blew the supervisor's mind. You know how them Christians are always worried about 666, when they should be more worried about helping us poor folks."

"Well, between 666 and 777, the Christians have their hands full, I suppose," said Aaron as he grinned at Joe. "I sometimes wonder which numbers are worse. 666 is the mark of the beast, but 777 deals with things the Christians treasure like the resurrection, spiritual completeness and the father's perfection. Yet, in my opinion, most of them show very little spiritual completeness and reflect almost none of the father's perfection when dealing with the less fortunate in our society or with those who do not fit their narrow-minded pattern of righteousness. I think if there is ever another appearance of their beloved, resurrected saviour, he will shake his head in shame at how they have perverted all that he stands for in a country that has made a hypocritical farce of his message."

Joe giggled out loud and said, "Damn if you ain't something Mr. Adams. You sure got them hypocrites' number. I just wish there were more people like you to stand up to 'um. This here country of ours is headed toward ruination cause it has been turned over to them and the rich to run as they please. People like me just don't mean anything to 'um. We just plain never did matter and never will."

"You got that right Joe. Getting back to the locket. I assume you sold it, too?"

"Sure did. Sold it to a Bandini family that lived over on High Street. I was glad to get rid of it. Just didn't feel right in my pocket. In fact, my pants got scorched on the inside of the pocket, and I had a little burn on my thigh that took years to go away. I ain't superstitious, but they did seem to be something about that there locket that just weren't natural."

Aaron stood up, thanked Joe, pulled out his wallet and took out three twenty dollar bills and placed them on the table.

"Thanks Mr. Adams. You are an all right guy. You are."

"You are pretty all right yourself Joe," said Aaron as he headed toward the door.

Joe whispered softly, "Be careful Mr. Adams. There is something just not right about all this. That locket is trouble. It just ain't an ordinary piece of jewellery."

"I'll be careful. That locket is certainly a harbinger of despair."

CHAPTER 10
PAIN AND EVIL OF THE VILEST FORM

Most things do not fall into place as easily as they had so far on this case. All Aaron had to do was back-trace the Bandini family now. No doubt, he would not be as lucky in finding them living in the same place they were over 50 years ago as he had been in finding a former employee at the thrift store.

Anyway, he decided to drop by and visit Rachael first. He caught the express IRT, and was at her door by 2:00 o'clock. No one answered the bell, as the place seemed deathly quiet, as quiet as a tomb. Even in the daylight, Hopkins House looked foreboding and evil. The curtains were drawn except for the small opening in the living room brocade drapes that let just a little light into the house. Aaron reflected back on how the light was so slight, but that it was just enough for him to see Rachael's magnificent V-mound between her legs that brought him such incredible pleasures. As he glared into the house through the small opening, he thought he saw a black figure move swiftly by the opening.

He knew the black figure was not Rachael's form, but he pulled the bell again anyway. He could not help but wonder if she was entertaining another gentleman caller. Was he jealous? Regardless, he pulled the door bell several more times, before giving up and heading back down the street. He had found the name Bandini in the Manhattan phone directory. He was heading over to High Street to see an Arturo Bandini.

Like so many other places in a country that always had to make room for more slums as its citizens descended from the middle class to poverty, High Street was now home to the poor and downtrodden. It was a place where those who had been left behind by the inhuman, uncaring capitalistic machinery of injustice struggled for a meagre existence and survival on the table scraps of arrogance tossed them by the rich and powerful.

The street was strewn with paper, broken bottles, beer cans, hypodermic needles and desperate, lost human beings. These people huddled in the doorways, alley-ways and vacant lots while their rich countrymen relaxed in their palatial, gated estates watching their large screen televisions and sipping dry martinis. Some of the rich and powerful might even ride through this part of town in their luxury cars with dark tinted windows on their way to plush upper Manhattan offices, without stopping to think about the obscene disparity between the rich and poor in a country that rewarded the rich and punished the poor and middle class.

Walking down the street made Aaron reflect on the immoral war that he was a part of years ago, and how so many of those who died came from slums like this. The people who were defending capitalism were the ones who had the least to gain from it. Hell, the poor suckers who were drafted, handed a gun and told to defend the American way, should have all taken their government issued rifles and joined the Viet Cong. They had a lot more in common with them than the rich, arrogant, self-righteous, flag-waving politicians who sent them to Vietnam to die while their own sons and daughters avoided the draft or were given slots in the National Guard. Wonder how many wars would occur if the President, the Cabinet members and Congress had to send their own sons and daughters to die for the war profiteers? Yet, the American public was too stupid to figure out that the government was not on their side. The government had only one purpose, to fuel the machinery of capitalism at all costs. The middle class and the poor were just the pawns that they manipulated into believing that they were living in a great, democratic society. What bullshit!

Looking at a dilapidated brownstone with a few boarded up windows, Aaron wondered if this was once the home of an affluent baron of greed who had deserted the neighbourhood when it started attracting an undesirable element. Then he saw a name carved in the stone above the oak door, Bandini.

Obviously, the Bandini family was far removed from this squalor and poverty now, but perhaps the resident would offer some clue to where they might be. Hell, the Bandini's might even be slum lords, renting this old home to those who had no choice but to live on this island of misery in a sea of plenty.

The bell was just like the one on Rachael's home. Aaron pulled on it several times, and he heard rustling inside. A short, nice-looking boy of about 25, with slightly crooked teeth opened the door. As Aaron looked down at him, he thought about other countries he had visited, like Sweden and Norway, where dental coverage was part of the free medical care available to all citizens. In those countries, you did not see children with crooked teeth, because the poor were afforded the same right to quality dental care that the rich were.

"Yes sir, what can I do for you," said the youth as he stuck out his woman-like chest and took a deep breath.

"I am Aaron Adams, and I am trying to locate a member of the Bandini family. I thought you might have an idea where I could find one of them."

Aaron knew his luck was holding when the boy smiled and said, "I am a Bandini, maybe I can help you."

"Well, I am delighted to hear that, but is there an older member of the family available? I think you might be a bit too young to be familiar with what I am looking for."

"Come in, my great-grandfather is here. Maybe he could help you. He is 88 years old."

"Thank you, I would love to talk to him."

The boy offered an extremely provocative smile, put up his right hand and motioned for Aaron to follow him into the house.

Aaron was slightly behind him as they meandered down the hall. The boy was extremely effeminate looking, and he had a very provocative sway to his hips. He kept looking over at Aaron and smiling. He actually winked at Aaron as they went into a musky, dirty looking room that was obviously a study.

"Wait here and I will get my great-grandfather."

As the boy left the room, he swayed his hips in an extreme manner and seemed to make himself very erect in stature, causing his ass to jut out profusely as he moved down the hall. Aaron thought to himself that the young boy would make a fine looking woman.

Aaron stood by some book shelves that were behind an old oak desk with several books on it. On the desk he noticed that whoever used the study obviously had a taste for socialism. Spread on the desk was a copy of Marx's *Das Kapital and Communist Manifesto*, both in German. He looked at a copy of *The Jungle* and thought back to his high school days when his English teacher made the class read Upton Sinclair's classic attack on capitalists in the meat packing industry who were willing to sell tainted meat and kill people in order to make a few extra cents per kilogram of beef.

As he peered at other books, he could not help but smile when he saw Che Guevara's *Motorcycle Diaries* and *Guerrilla Warfare*, two books that had been banned in America for years. Seeing Mao's *Little Red Book* opened to page 36 made Aaron remember that he had kept a copy of this Communist Bible on his desk at the Pentagon, where he was stationed after returning from Vietnam. Many times generals had come through his office and made disparaging remarks when they saw it on his desk. Originally, he had just kept it there to irritate the higher echelon who talked about defending freedom, then had the gall to attack a soldier for practicing the freedom to read whatever he wanted. Then, he actually read the book and saw the beauty in the words written by a man who believed in equality for all men by protecting them from capitalistic exploitation. That was the beginning of his transformation. It was Mao's writings that helped him see the hypocrisy of an America that preached democracy, but practiced totalitarian subjugation of all its citizens to capitalistic greed.

Lost in deep thought, Aaron snapped back to the reality of the moment when he heard a voice say, "I am Arturo Bandini. I believe you want to see me?"

Turning around, Aaron came face to face with a tall, robust looking older gentleman who exhibited an air of authority. Shocked at the quietness of his entrance into the room, Aaron's voiced quivered a bit when he said, "Yes, I am Aaron Adams, and I am trying to locate a locket for a client. It appears that many years ago the Bandini family possessed this locket."

Ignoring the statement about the locket, the old gentleman said, "I see you are interested in my reading material."

"Yes, very much so. I have read all the books on your desk; although I read the English version of *Das Kapital* and *The Communist Manifesto*."

Smiling Arturo Bandini said, "It is nice to know that there are still some among the younger generation who seek out knowledge of better systems of economic justice than our old, sick, tired method of greed and institutionalized poverty."

"Sir, I see the results of greed everyday in a city where the rich and powerful look with disdain on those who have been marginalized by the greed and avarice living of the privileged class."

"Spoken like a true socialist my boy. You and I are a dying breed, I fear."

"I am not sure what I am, sir. I do know what I am not. I am not a supporter of the cult of greed represented by Ronald Reagan and his band of robber barons."

Warming to the conversation, Arturo Bandini eased into his old leather chair behind the desk and motioned for Aaron to have a seat on a well-worn Queen Anne chair.

Scratching his bald pate, the old gentleman leaned back in his chair and said, "So, you are not here to discuss politics, but to find an object of great importance to someone. I thought the Hopkins family had turned to dust long ago after they were all killed in the horrible nightmare that brought an end to the Harry Hopkins' empire of greed and rapacity. Surely, it must be some distant relative who desires the object."

"Well, I am not sure how distant a relative my client is, but she does wish to retrieve the locket for personal reasons."

The old man leaned forward, cupped his hands and rested his chin on them. "I know the locket Mr. Adams. I know it well. I am afraid my wife bought that infernal thing in 1925 from an old drunk who worked at the Salvation Army. I knew from the time that it arrived this family was destined for tragedy. It was a day in the fall of 1925. My wife was all excited about the good deal she got on such a marvellous piece of jewellery. Mr. Adams, you are looking at an atheist who sees religion as nothing but a method of mass societal control and manipulation. I believe more in *Mother Goose* nursery rhymes than I do in the ridiculous stories in the Bible, which, were all written many hundreds of years before the Bible in other texts. Even the prototype of Jesus appears as a God in ancient Egyptian mythology. Yet, as a thoroughly rational man who thinks of himself as too intelligent to fall for Biblical tall tales, I took one look at that locket which was warm to the touch, and I saw the numbers 666. I looked at my wife's hands which were slightly burned, and I told her to get rid of the thing, immediately."

Aaron was astonished at his luck on this case. Two visits to different people and they both had knowledge of the locket. He crossed his legs and urged the old gentleman to continue his story.

"Well, there is a great deal to tell, but I will shorten it as much as possible. After all, at my age, time is of the essence. We both tried to pry it open to no avail. Whatever was inside the locket was to remain a mystery, because it seemed to be sealed shut. My wife insisted that the locket was a perfect gift for her sister. Hell, I never liked the old bitch anyway, so I figure what the shit. Let the self-righteous Christian asshole have it. I assumed she would not take it anyway, because once she saw the 666 on the locket, she would invoke the name of Jesus to rid her of evil. She would probably throw it in my wife's face and accuse her of bringing the devil into the house."

"However, I was surprised when her sister started wearing it. It was not long until she complained of a rash around her neck, which she assumed was because the chain was not pure silver. The rich old bitch thought she should have the best of everything. It was only a few weeks when evil seemed to permeate this house which we shared with my wife's bitch sister. Fortunately, my son was away at boarding school, but here in the house all sorts of terrible things started to happen. The water main broke and flooded the house. We had a fire in the upper floors. The sewer backed up. A stairwell railing broke, and my wife fell to her death. I will never forget the look of terror she had on her face. Too this day, I am convinced she did not fall from the stairs. I sincerely think she saw somebody or something that frightened her so much that she fell against the railing and broke it as a result of fear. Her right hip was facing up when she was found, but it had a severe bruise on it, almost as if she had been hit in the hip with an object. But this was only the beginning. Two months later, my wife's sister, Jesus lover that she was, committed suicide by falling on a butcher knife, dying an excruciatingly painful death."

"Again, Mr. Adams, I am not a man who believes in any of the mumbo jumbo of an obvious work of fiction conjured up by a pack of self-serving old men who are responsible for the enslavement of almost one-half of humanity to the idea of exclusionary religious bigotry that sits idly by while millions suffer from capitalistic exploitation, but when I saw the locket placed on the bureau in my sister-in-law's room, and under it written on a small piece of paper the word "evil", I knew that there had to be something unexplainable that had brought all the misery to this house. I put the locket in my pants pocket, and vowed that I would find out to whom it originally belonged, and return the evil thing posthaste."

"However, I let the locket languish in the pocket as other things took priority. You see, my son, who had come home from boarding school, as a result of his mother's death, begged me not to send him back to boarding school. Being a different man at the time, one who was, unfortunately, a member of the capitalist class, I was convinced that my son should not mingle with the common children who were in public schools. I am afraid that I was like many of the parents today who think their children will be corrupted as a result of exposure to the common classes. However, I am proud to say that he was not in a religious boarding school, where he would have been taught to be judgmental and hypocritical."

Aaron could not resist chirping in, "Yes, religious education is at the very heart of our judgmental society that spends too much time pointing the finger of condemnation, when it should be embracing humanity with compassion and understanding."

The old man continued, "Fortunately, the boy was a person of immense wisdom for his young age, and of a nobler mind than his father at the time. He insisted that he should go to public school, as he was no better than the maid's son who toiled for us to support her family that had been left destitute after having lost her home to pay her dead husband's hospital bills."

Aaron smiled, looked the old gentleman directly in the eyes and said, "Sounds like he was a man of the people. Obviously, based upon the literature on the desk, you came around to his way of thinking."

"That I did Mr. Adams. That I did. I wasted many years in the pursuit of wealth in a society that has one God above all others, money. I should have pursued social and economic justice, something that is sorely lacking in a world ruled by the corporate robber barons that now have a front man in the White House. Ronald Reagan is the poster boy for mediocrity, but mark my words, that Bush character he has for Vice-President, along with the rest of the Nazi-like clique now running the country, will one day form a cabal of banality that will drag this nation into the deepest pit of malice and corporate malfeasance imaginable. Thankfully, I will not be around to see it."

Warming to the prophecies of future political evil, Aaron interjected, "Well, I am only 35 and I have already seen enough political chicanery to last a life time. The Republicans are in the pockets of big business and the religious bigots. Yet, the Democrats do not offer much of an alternative; although, they do look after the middle class and poor on occasion. I am sure you are proud of your son for standing tall against the hypocrisy of the elite."

"More proud of him that if he had been President of the USA. In 1958, at the age of 44 he went to school in Mexico to learn Spanish, so he could join Fidel Castro and Che Guevara to rid Cuba of that American corporate backed despot, Batista."

A tear formed in the old man's right eye, and as he wiped it away he said, "He was killed defending the revolution at the Bay of Pigs, still fighting alongside Fidel Castro, who personally led the fight against the CIA backed counterrevolutionaries. Can you imagine that boob in the White House now, who spent World War II in the USO, showing up at the beaches to defend America from invaders? He would be scurrying out the backdoor of the White House while telling the poor to get their guns and defend the American way."

Aaron could not help but laugh out loud. He had seen the same thing in Vietnam. The poor were sent to defend capitalism, while the sons of those who benefited the most from it, were not in Vietnam fighting for their country. They were safely ensconced in the National Guard or graduate school.

No matter how much Aaron enjoyed getting off the subject, he felt compelled to steer the old man's meandering ramblings on social justice back to the subject which was of paramount interest to Aaron at the time. "I enjoy the political discussions Mr. Bandini, but I do need to know about the locket."

"Sorry Mr. Adams, I do often get overly passionate about social ills when it would be so easy to take care of them if we would just stop spending money on bombs and tax breaks for the rich and put it to good use for a change. Anyway, my son, in 1925, refused to go back to boarding school in Connecticut, so I enrolled him in PS935 over near Broadway and Sasson. Several times I received a message from the school principal that he was continuously showing up late for school. He always left the house very early, so rather than confront him with the miscreant deed he was supposed to be committing, I elected to follow him to school in the mornings. Upon doing so, I immediately noticed that he went considerably out of his way to go to school."

The old man scratched his head and continued. "I followed him several days at a considerable distance to avoid detection. He was cutting through back alleys, and each day he would wind up on Farragut Street. Each day he stopped in front of Hopkins House."

Aaron sat up straighter in his chair as his interest was piqued.

Arturo Bandini saw he had struck a cord that was music to Aaron's ears. "Each day he stood there at the bottom of the steps, just looking up at the door until an extremely handsome, robust looking woman would open the door, descend the stairs and whisper something to him."

The old man got up from his chair, walked to the bookshelf and pulled out an ancient-looking book, opening it to the middle. He removed an old, stained, worn part of a newspaper page, walked over and handed it to Aaron. "Read the last paragraph Mr. Adams."

Being careful not to tear the tattered clipping, Aaron scanned down the page to the last paragraph and read it. *"Although it appears that this is an obvious case of a woman gone mad, there is a neighbour who claims to have seen a gentleman arguing vociferously with the assumed murderer, Candace Hopkins, the day before. If any of our readers has information in regards to the unknown man, please contact the police."*

Aaron offered the paper back to Arturo Bandini, but with a wave of the right hand, he told Aaron. "Keep it, you may find the rest of the article interesting."

Putting the clipping in his coat breast pocket, Aaron asked Arturo, "And what is the significance of the last paragraph to what I am trying to find, Mr. Bandini?"

Smiling as he made his way back to his chair, easing into it, Arturo replied, "The gentleman arguing with Candace was me."

Aaron eyes grew larger and his demeanour took on a more determined look. "You knew Candace Hopkins?"

"I met the woman once. It was on the very day that she murdered the entire family. You see, we were not arguing, she was just upset and demanding I return something to her."

A smile gradually swept across Aaron's face, "the locket."

"Yes, Mr. Adams. She was demanding the return of the locket. You see, my son had met one of the Hopkins women by chance at the funeral of my beloved wife. It was she who had him come by Hopkins House on a regular basis. It seems she was aware that the locket had wound up in our household. It was my son who told me that she encouraged him to search for it, and to return it to her. The day I asked him about his visits to Hopkins House, he told me the truth. I had forgotten what I did with the locket as grief had overwhelmed me. She was incensed when I told her I had no idea where the locket was. I refused to discuss it any further. I turned and left as she continued to shout vindictive tirades at me. Obviously, a neighbour had seen the exchange between us, and I was mentioned in the paper."

"Mr. Bandini, do you have the locket?"

"I wish I could help you Mr. Adams, but years after the incident, the locket disappeared from this house. I have no idea where it is. Believe me; I would love to help you, because that thing is the very essence of evil. I do believe that with all my heart. I know of the rumours about Hopkins House. I do believe there is something sinister and evil about that infernal place. What it has to do with the locket I do not know, but whatever it is, the evil will never rest until the house is gone. I sometimes wish I had the courage to burn it to the ground. Yet, I fear that the evil is so pervasive that it might survive even that."

"Have you looked for the locket in a judicious manner over the years?"

"Mr. Adams, I have never ceased to look for it. My son and a grandson have died, and each time I felt that it might have had something to do with that locket, so I continued to look for it. I fear for my great grandson's life.

The old gentleman shook his head. "I love my great grandson very much, so I have never told him of my fears. His own father died in this house, in almost the same manner as his great grandmother. I sincerely believe my son would have died here, too, had he not been killed in Cuba. Why I have been spared I do not know, unless it is to punish me by letting me live to see all my progeny wiped from the face of the earth."

Again a tear streamed down his cheek as he looked directly at Aaron. "I know my great grandson is a bit out of the norm. He dresses like a woman, and he meets men often. I know that the Bandini name dies with him regardless of what happens, because he will never have any children. I can live with that, just as long as I know he is safe. I sincerely hope that I die before he does, because I could not bear to lose another loved one."

"That does not make him abnormal my dear Mr. Bandini. I learned long ago that what is between a person's legs does not always define gender. As long as he carries the compassionate Bandini gene, you should be proud of him. That is the real measure of a person's worth in a world that shows no compassion, warmth or understanding."

"You are a man of infinite wisdom Mr. Adams. I wish I had known you back when. At the end of my life I find fewer and fewer genuinely compassionate individuals who see through the façade of our society that breeds contempt for all who dare to be different. Like McDonalds that homogenizes all their restaurants with sameness, our society also celebrates sameness with its complete lack of originality. I am afraid we are a country headed down the path of fascism as surely as I am headed for the grave."

"Mr. Bandini, you have saddened me with your tales of woe and your inability to find the locket, but you have brightened my day by showing me that there are still those who seek justice in a country that has none. I salute you and all you stand for in a society that is dragging the entire world to the evil of greedy, self-serving, uncaring capitalism."

Arturo got up from his chair, walked over and embraced Aaron. Aaron could smell snuff on him. It reminded Aaron of the wonderful smell of his grandmother who had been his rock in a sea of turmoil during his childhood. The wrinkled old body gave Aaron a feeling of warmth and security. He hated to leave. He felt a kinship with this old gentleman, and he knew that he would forever remember this meeting as one of the highlights of his life. Here was a man who cared. While most people became insular and conservative in old age, this man had opened up his mind, and more importantly, his heart to the possibilities of mankind. It was too bad that he lived in a society where kindness, caring, justice and acceptance were scarce commodities.

As they moved toward the door, Aaron glanced down the hallway and saw the young boy had put on makeup, a tight mini-skirt and bright red lipstick. Smiling, he waved at him and nodded his approval. The boy smiled back and there was an instant simpatico. They understood each other. If only all of society could reach such an understanding of acceptance and respect.

Again embracing at the front door, Aaron was surprised when the old man, while saying good-bye uttered a warning, "Be careful my son, be careful of the evil in Hopkins House. I believe in the ancient myth of *Ju On*, and if ever there was a place where evil spirits would reside, it is within the walls of Hopkins House. It is a place that knows pain and evil of the vilest form."

CHAPTER 11
A USELESS INSTRUMENT IN HOPKINS HOUSE

As the sun descended behind the horizon, Aaron could not help but dread meeting Rachael with the news that he still had been unable to locate the locket. After opening the door, all his trepidation disappeared as Rachael reached out with her somewhat cold hand, took him down the hallway, into the living room and started removing her clothes without saying a word. It was done in one swift motion as she undid the spaghetti strap over her right shoulder and the dress fell to the floor, crumbling up at her feet. She had nothing else on.

Standing before him in all her magnificent glory, Aaron was mesmerized by her sexual boldness. The thick, seemingly never ending hair, glistening with perspiration, on her mound of desire stretched right up to her rounded, slightly protruding, sexy stomach. The blackness of it against her somewhat pale skin made Aaron gasp for breath as he reached out to touch it, to feel the very blackness, to feel the sexual energy that seemed to emanate from within her soul. As she bent down to unzip his pants, Aaron sighed with delight while reaching for the back of her head, gently caressing her soft, thick, silky mane. Dropping his pants to the floor, she got up and removed his shirt and tie. Still not saying a word, she again knelt before him, removing his briefs and then she began to rhythmically work on his manhood with her mouth like a conductor wrapped up in the rhapsody of a symphony. The music swelled in Aaron's ears as the ecstasy of the moment overwhelmed him.

Finally, Rachael stood before him and Aaron wrapped her in his arms as their lips met in a long, passionate kiss. The silence was finally broken when Rachael looked into Aaron's eyes and pulled him onto the sofa on top of her. She put her hands behind her head, exposing her hairy underarms. Aaron blew softly on the hair, then kissed it, burying his face into it as he said, "Rachael, I am overwhelmed with passion and love."

With tears swelling in her eyes and her voice quivering, Rachael said, "My dearest Aaron. I, too, love you passionately. How I wish we could be together forever. This moment will be with me in eternity as I reflect back on how we shared this interlude of unbridled love and passion."

Squirming her way from under Aaron, she went to the end of the sofa, laying her torso down over the thick padded arm and resting her head in the musky cushion of the sofa, she exposed her derriere and squirmed. Aaron, knowing what she desired, slowly moved toward her. She reached back with both hands and spread her cheeks. Aaron moved forward and their bodies became one as they lost themselves in the harmonious ecstasy of the moment. Losing all track of time, it was as if they had floated upward from the confines of earth to heavenly bliss as this one moment became a lifetime.

Wrapped in each others arms, they lay on the floor, basking in the afterglow of the most glorious sex imaginable. Totally spent from the frenzy of unbridled passion, they did not speak. Words were not necessary to show the intense feelings that had developed between them. Together, they were as one now. Yet, Aaron felt a distance between them. There seemed to be something that Rachael was not sharing. She had confided so much to him, but what was it that made Aaron feel that she was holding something back, something that might alter their relationship.

Turning on her side and smiling, Rachael seemed content as she said, "Aaron, my darling, you do not know how long it has been since a man has made me feel like this. You have brought great pleasure to a woman who has been trapped in misery for too long now. Each day I reside here in this den of inequity and evil, I seem to drift deeper into despair and hopelessness. You are my only salvation. You are the only hope I have of freeing myself from the bonds that bind me to the past, a past that will not let me go."

"Rachael, I am here to serve you. I long to make your life what it should be. You are in my thoughts constantly, and I long to give you what you need. Yet, I have been unable to find the locket, but I vow that it will be found, regardless of my personal belief that it is not that infernal trinket that brings the evil to this house."

Standing up, Rachael turned her back to Aaron, and he noticed that the white, gooey residue of his passion oozed from between her magnificent ass cheeks. She smiled, looked over her shoulder and squeezed her cheeks together by tightening her muscles. "I don't want to lose one bit of you. I want to keep your warmth in me forever."

Aaron stood, his manhood on the rise again as Rachael turned to face him. "Dearest Rachael, I am now forever a part of you. You will never be able to free yourself from me."

Putting her dress back on, Rachael's countenance became more serious, "Aaron, if only that could be true. You are the most precious man I have ever known, but I am afraid there is something that will always keep us apart. No matter how much love there is between us, I am forever trapped within the confines of a house that reeks with the very essence of evil, unless I find that locket."

As Aaron leisurely dressed, suddenly a noise came from the upper floor. Aaron looked at Rachael. She looked back and shook her head. "Do not be alarmed. It is the time of night that the evil walks about in pursuit of release from the confines of the walls that imprison the spirits that seek freedom from their torment. The only hope for them is the locket."

"I need the chance to examine this so-called evil. You must allow me to enter into that infernal room that you are so convinced harbours the evil. I need to see where the massacre occurred and this evil supposedly incubated and grew."

Rachael was waiting for Aaron now. She did not say a word; she just stood there, waiting for him to follow her into the darkness that harboured the evil in Hopkins House. Moving into the hallway, then up the stairs, she stopped on the landing outside the second floor bedroom of the youngest sister. It was then that she broke the silence. "This is a room that served as a catalyst for much of what occurred here. Although, I do not believe there was any inherent evil in the sexual escapades of the youngest Hopkins sister. After all, sex is not much more than a recreational activity, right my dearest."

Smiling broadly, Aaron replied, "Well, sex is definitely my favourite recreational activity. Based upon what I have read and heard about the three sisters, I would think this house has seen its share of sexual activity."

The smile gradually disappearing from her face, Rachael looked upward as the muffled sound of footsteps filtered down from the third floor. "Are you sure you want to do this Aaron. I do not think it is a good idea."

"Rachael, I need to see for myself what you are so fearful of in this house."

They held hands as Rachael led Aaron up the stairs toward the third floor. They stopped and stood on the landing that led into the room of infamy, preparing to face the evil that had for so long plagued Hopkins House.

They were silent as a faint moaning sound penetrated through the closed door. The dark was pervasive and the blackness of the landing seemed to swirl around them. They both appeared to be glued in their tracks, fearful that a movement forward would doom them to an everlasting hell. Yet, the room seemed to be beckoning them, and they could not resist its call. They moved forward very slowly. Aaron's breathing quickened, but Rachael seemed more relaxed and at ease.

The dark waited, waited for Aaron to enter the portal of evil. The house was alive, not with the living, but with the dead. As Aaron pushed on the giant oak door that opened into the bedroom, he knew that what was waiting for him was too sinister for the mind of a mortal to comprehend. The deaths that had occurred here were a testament to the evil that embraced darkness like a long lost friend. The dark seemed to creep beneath the door as he gingerly pushed inward, thinking about all that had led to this moment, a moment when he would have to come face to face with something evil in the darkness at Hopkins House.

For nearly sixty years the room harboured evil. Five people had been killed as a result of the evil emanating from this four walled hell. Rachael begged Aaron, in a quite womanly way, to wait until the morning, when there would be no danger, and then he could enter the room unencumbered with the fear of facing the evil that only seemed to present itself in the dark.

The moaning noises ceased as Aaron completely opened the door. Standing in the doorway, Aaron surveyed the scene, and saw that the room was empty, at least empty of any flesh and blood mortal. However, it did seem to have a certain life to it. There was an indescribable feeling of dread about the place. There was sadness to the room, as if it was desolate and lonely.

Rachael, quickly closing the door behind them said, "They must never leave this room as the evil will permeate the entire house, engulfing all within its power. They long to do so, but there is something that keeps them within. I suggest keeping the door closed, because if they are released into the house, they will refuse to return. Yet, there is one thing that will release them, let them leave this place of unmitigated mischief and calamity once and for all. The locket, the locket opened so that the demon can find its way home. Once the demon is gone, so will the curse of evil be gone, obliterated for once and all from this den of inequity."

The room was furnished in grand style, with a huge four-poster bed, which stood with its head to the end wall. There was a lamp on the mantelpiece, and one on each of the two tables that were in the room. Aaron motioned for Rachael to turn on some lights and their glow made the room less inhumanly dreary.

Aaron took a good look around and walked over to the windows. He checked to make sure they were securely closed and locked. They appeared to have not been raised in decades as there was much dust and debris around the sills. All the time, as he walked about the room, Rachael just stood by the bed.

Finally, Rachael whispered, "You do not realize the danger of this room. You should not be here. Only the ghosts of the past are welcome within."

Aaron could see that Rachael was not fearful for herself. It was he she feared for in this place of evil. All the same, Aaron continued to survey the room until he came to the infamous spot on the wall. Looking at it, he turned to Rachael. Pointing at the spot he said, "You expect me to believe that spot harbours a demon?"

"I expect you to be careful and not question that which you do not understand or believe. Just be assured that only one thing can bring an end to evil here. It is the locket. Please Aaron, please do not tempt this room. It is alive with evil. I know it, but I do not want to prove it to you. You are not safe here in this place of evil."

"Rachael, I am going to ask you to leave tonight. Leave me alone in this room to face this perceived evil. I am going to prove that all this is nothing more than the result of furtive imaginations. Go down stairs and get masking tape or cellophane tape for me."

Confused as to why Aaron wanted tape, Rachael did not question him; she just did as he asked. Upon her return with the masking tape, Aaron proceeded to stretch it across the spot on the wall, extending it horizontally, then crossing it vertically, so that the merest touch would break it, if anyone or anything were to venture into the room in the dark unseen or unheard. He also placed tape around the windows and wardrobe. When the clock struck twelve, Aaron turned his back to the door and had a seat. He asked Rachael to leave. She kissed him on the head while his back was still turned to the door. He heard her gently walk across the floor, and just as he turned toward the door, he was shocked to see that she was already gone, as if she had just disappeared into thin air.

Aaron took off his coat, laid it on the bed and walked across to a chair, and picked it up. He was in the act of putting it against the wall to face the door when he heard a low whisper from the opposite corner of the room. He could not make out what was said, but it was a whisper. Of that he was certain.

At exactly the same time, one of the three lamps went out. There also seemed to be a cold breeze in the room, and Aaron became a bit apprehensive as he saw mist come out of his mouth. The room was getting colder. He actually considered making a run for the door, but decided that his mind was just playing tricks on him. Most people would say not to fear the dead, only fear the living. Yet, Aaron had learned in Vietnam that the dead could be deadly. Many enemy soldiers booby trapped themselves, so that in case they were killed, the Americans would touch them and set off explosives. There were numerous times Aaron had seen the dead commit acts of deadly mayhem. Respect for the dead was something Aaron had learned the hard way. Although he did not believe in ghosts, he did believe in the power of evil. Every day he saw the evil of a society based on greed. The homeless, the slaving minorities and the faceless masses who struggled for survival were a testament to the evil that permeated a corrupt, uncaring society.

Boldly Aaron moved toward the two lamps still brightly lighting the room and turned them off. He was bathing himself in darkness. If there was something evil in the room he would meet it on its own terms. He would not be deterred from his quest to explore the depths of evil in Hopkins House.

Aaron made for the door, and had to muster a bit of courage not to start running. He took some thundering long strides, and as he stood by the oak door he had a sudden feeling that there was a cold wind in the room. It was almost as if the window had been suddenly opened.

He instinctively put his hand on the doorknob, and started to turn it. However, something inside him told him not to give into fear. This was something he had to do. Whatever was in this room would know that Aaron was as determined as it was. He removed his hand from the knob and placed tape across the door frame.

He moved through the dark toward the bed that was partially visible due to the moonlight that was filtering into the room. He moved his coat to the far side of the bed and lay down. The smell of the musty bed penetrated his nostrils and he wondered where Rachael slept. Obviously, no one had slept in this room for years.

Aaron closed his eyes and tried to sleep. Just as he dosed off he heard a loud crash somewhere near the spot on the wall. He sat up in bed, and listened, but heard nothing else. Then he reached in his pocket and brought out the pen knife with a light in it. Just as he was turning on a light there came a pounding of the door. He jumped out of bed, and pulled his big bastard of a 45 out of his shoulder holster. He stood there by the bed, shinning the light toward the door. As he started to move toward the door he seemed to freeze in his tracks. Try as hard as he could, his feet seemed immobilized. There was something in the air, something indiscernibly evil.

Then Aaron sat on the edge of the bed, and listened to the dismal low whimpering sound that seemed to come from the far wall where the spot was. The whimpering seemed to echo throughout the room. He wondered if Rachael was alright. Had she heard the commotion coming from the room, but out of deference to her new found lover's request, avoided disturbing him in his pursuit of the spirits that haunted Hopkins House?

Aaron could not explain why. He did not see it, but he felt it. Yes, to the very fibre of his being, he felt there was something in the room with him. The blackness surrounded him, but suddenly the feeling of evil was gone. There was a serenity that engulfed the room, a quiet, loving serenity. Yes, love was the word. Aaron felt love in the room. Then he heard the voice of a woman, a low, husky voice that seemed to be filled with love. He could hardly make out what was being said as a cold wind gradually swirled about and the feeling began to change. The whispering voice of the woman faded toward the wall, the last word he heard was "you." What was she trying to tell him?

The feeling changed abruptly. There was still someone or something in the room, but now there was an overpowering feeling of evil. The breeze grew colder and colder. The lights faded. Aaron looked at his jacket he had folded up on the bed. It had been rumpled up and thrown over the head board.

Shining his pin light toward the far wall, he thought he caught a glimpse of a black object seeming to dissipate before his eyes. There had been something evil in the room. Aaron knew that, but what was it? He was not ready to believe in ghosts. Was his mind playing tricks on him?

With the room still bathed in darkness, Aaron looked at his watch. It was 1:15. Keeping his gun in his right hand and penlight in his left, Aaron lay back down, and stared at the ceiling. He heard a faint sound coming from the far wall, and got up to get a closer look, being careful not to make too much noise, almost as if he did not want to disturb the demon.

Aaron stood there, looking at the wall that was clearly visible in the moonlight that danced through the window now, almost as if something outside had ordained that the light be provided so he could get a good look at the wall. Suddenly a cloud gradually crossed in front of the moon, again bathing the room in darkness.

Aaron heard a faint noise near the door. At the same time, he was conscious of a queer prickling sensation about the back of his neck, and his hands began to sweat. The following instant, the whole room appeared to whirl about and there was a pounding sound that made the room seem to shake. The oak door started to vibrate as if something or someone was desperately trying to open it.

The thud, thud, thud, thud pounded into Aaron's brain. Then a silence that was almost worse than the noise came abruptly, and Aaron found himself wanting to fire his weapon to wipe out the silence that was so loud it nearly shattered his eardrums.

Moving to the bed, he sat down on the soft mattress and sank deeply into it. With a revolver in one hand and a penlight in the other, he just sat there staring into the darkness. He looked at the revolver in his hand, and wondered what good was it? It was a useless instrument in Hopkins House.

CHAPTER 12
PUTTING GHOSTS TO REST IN HOPKINS HOUSE

Aaron was a sceptic about everything in life. The Bible to him was nothing more than a book of fairy tales that people accepted as gospel, because they had never taken the time to read the exact same stories that had been written in ancient times and recorded in other texts or had been passed on by oral tradition. He never believed anything that emanated from the mouths of hypocritical politicians who used patriotism as a way to control and manipulate the citizens of a country filled with mindless sheep who were willing die for an idea that did not really exist. He always saw through the corporate thievery that used public relations to convince the people that big companies always had the consumers' best interests in mind. He scoffed at a military that had sent him to defend so-called freedom while it was the instrument of oppression in country after country that wanted to throw off the yoke of capitalistic domination by American corporations. Very little in life escaped Aaron's critical eye. That is why it was so hard for him to accept what he had experienced in Hopkins House that night. He still did not believe in ghosts, but he could not deny what had occurred during that eventful night. Was he, like so many people in America, just another victim of mass hypnotism by those who used deceit and lies to promulgate their power base? Yet, what would anyone have to gain by him believing in ghosts. There was no pot of gold at the end of the rainbow in this case.

The darkness was still about Aaron, and he was determined that he would not shirk from the task at hand. He looked around at the big, empty room. Then he had an abrupt, extraordinary sense of weirdness thrust upon him in the form of a smell. In the air, there was a sense of something inhuman impending. The room was full of the stench of decaying flesh which Aaron had sniffed so often in Vietnam, when he and his fellow soldiers were hungering down, avoiding detection by the enemy as his fellow soldiers lay in the jungle rot dying.

He recalled that smell with horror, and the many times he heard young boys as they were dying calling out for their mothers. He began to cry uncontrollably as he reflected back on those days of terror which were much worse than anything he had experienced in Hopkins House. He recalled his buddy from school, Charles from Asheboro, North Carolina, who only a few days before he was due to come back home, bent down to tie his shoes and was killed by an explosion. He thought back on how he and Charles had played together as children, and how America had demanded they serve in an immoral war meant to perpetuate capitalist domination of a poor country that only wanted to be left alone to decide its own destiny. He wiped his tears and looked over at the door. He began to see a kaleidoscope of his early life as if it was being flashed on a movie screen. There was his dad, whom he adored so much, standing with his arm around a six year old Aaron, taking time to play with him in one of the few moments he had for his son. He recalled how his father always said he was building an empire for his children, but Aaron did not want an empire, all he wanted was warmth and love from his father. In the end, Aaron left his hometown behind, and journeyed about the country in search of solace and compassion, until he finally settled on Long Island and found a mentor to teach him the private eye business.

As he continued to cry, he saw the kaleidoscope gradually dissipate. He briefly closed his eyes and it was gone. This house was playing tricks on his mind, just as it did the first day he laid eyes on it, when he saw visions of his father in that old, dilapidated building. He wiped his eyes and sat there staring at the door, as if he was waiting for someone or something to walk through it.

He had no idea what horrible thing was going to walk through that door. He could not forget that five people had met their deaths in Hopkins House, four of them within the confines of the horrid room in which he sat mesmerized with consternation.

This was the most dangerous and baffling case he had ever investigated. Yet, he had found Rachael, so the danger was a small price to pay for the affection and love of such a wonderful woman.

He found himself glancing over his shoulder, constantly, and then all around the room. It was unnerving, awaiting the arrival of a ghost or ghosts. Then, suddenly, he was aware of a mild, cold breeze sweeping over him, coming from behind. He twisted his body around, and stared straight into the cold breeze. It seemed to come from the corner of the room to the left of the bed. Yet, he could see nothing unusual; the darkness appeared to swirl about the room, almost like a whirlpool.

Sitting in the darkness, Aaron felt helpless. He thought back to Vietnam, when in the dark, the quiet would be more frightening than the sounds of bombs and bullets. The quiet was deadly in Nam. The quiet was your enemy. The quiet harboured the deadly evil of the night, just waiting to overwhelm you and pull you into that dark pit that was below that horrible precipice upon which all of humanity teeters.

A time of abominable tenseness passed, and still the slight cold breeze blew upon him. Suddenly, in the pitch black, near the infamous spot on the wall, something stirred, making a sound like a whisper. Aaron was made conscious of it by some inward, unused sense than transcended sight and sound; something woefully out of the normal. As he stared into the blackness, something began slowly to grow in the front of the wall. It was not a being; rather it was a moving shadow, a little darker than the surrounding shadows. He lost the thing amid the vagueness, and for a moment or two, glanced swiftly from side to side, with a fresh, new sense of impending danger. Then he stood up. Squinting his eyes, he desperately tried to locate the shadow again. Just as he took a step forward, he heard a faint noise behind him. He turned and looked down at the bed. The duvet was slowly and methodically being pulled off toward the

the foot of the bed into the darkness by some unseen hand. He listened intently to the slow dragging of the material, but he could see nothing at the foot of the bed. Then he looked down toward the edge of the footboard and thought he saw a shadow in the shape of a hand. He immediately became aware in a subconscious, introspective fashion that the fright of what was happening sent shivers through his body. His mental state was alert, but he was trapped in a comatose state, as he could not move or react in any fashion.

The sweating in his left hand nearly made him drop the revolver. He quickly shifted it to his right hand, wiping the left hand on his shirt. Through it all, he never moved and never shifted his gaze or his attention from the moving duvet.

The faint noises from the bed ceased, and there was a most intense silence, with only the sound of Aaron's heavy breathing penetrating the darkness. The duvet was now crumpled up at the foot of the bed. Whatever had been there was apparently gone.

There was absolute quietness for a couple of minutes. Abruptly, over by the door, Aaron heard a faint noise - a sort of crackling sound, and then the soft steps of two feet upon the floor. A nervous anxiety swept over him, seeming to run up his spine and the back of his neck. Something was there. The intense dark kept him from seeing the door. He thought to himself how much was he actually seeing, and how much was he imagining. It seemed that something dark and indistinct moved and wavered there by the door as if blocking his exit. Abruptly, there was a moan from the area that was hollow and wispy. It grew loud and thunderous, as if something was crying out with intense pain and anguish, almost pleading for release. There seemed such a longing to the sound, a vast, wanton force that was not malevolent, but was pleading. No, it was begging, begging for something unknown, but what could it want. What could this thing want from a mortal? What desires and longings forced it to moan forlornly in the depths of darkness at Hopkins

House?

From the opposite side of the room there rose suddenly a hideous caterwaul, that ceased abruptly; and then, Aaron looked toward the window and he could see the moonlight cast an eerie glow on a greyish-black cat that was peering in the window. The window slowly began to rise, as if lifted by an invisible hand. Aaron noticed a dark shadow to the right side of the window. The cat started to leap from the ledge as the window was obscured from view when a cloud crept over the moon, blotting out the light. Screeching furiously, as it tried to get away, Aaron could tell that the cat was being pulled into the room. Aaron heard a loud whine and the cat immediately ceased making noises. It was dead. Aaron knew whatever was near the window had killed the cat. The cat's body was flung across the room, hitting the far wall with a resounding thud.

He saw nothing else, but he was full with the knowledge that he was in the presence of some being or thing that had the power to destroy. During the next few seconds, there was an odd, noticeable fluttering sound all about the room, and Aaron whirled around, trying to see whether anything was coming at him. He expected to be attacked by one or more evil beings at anytime.

As his eyes became adjusted to the dark, power of sight came gradually, and he noticed a big, indistinct, wavering blackness in the corner of the room near the window. It appeared as though the shadow of a vast spider hung suspended in the air, just beyond his reach. It seemed to move forward toward Aaron, only to draw back with extraordinary jerky movements.

It moved toward the ceiling and hovered. Then it came straight toward him, appearing to gather form and solidity as it came forward and downward. There seemed a vast, malign determination behind the movement that must succeed. Aaron was on his knees, and he jerked back, falling on to his left hand,

and hip, in a wild endeavour to get back from the advancing evil incarnation. With his right hand grabbing madly for his revolver that had fallen to the floor, the brutal thing came with one great sweep straight overhead. Then, just as suddenly as it had swept over, it seemed to be hurled back by some mighty, invisible force. Aaron thought he heard a soft feminine voice in almost a whisper say, "Do not hurt the mortal."

For what seemed like an eternity he concentrated on what he thought was a hand beckoning in the darkness ; but, presently, he thought he saw, once or twice, an odd wavering, over among the shadows near the door. A little later, as though in a sudden fit of malignant rage, a whispering voice, indistinguishable, seemed to be arguing with someone or something.

Shortly, the door was pounded on with tremendous force. The next instant one of two shadows made one swift, vicious dart at him from out of the darkness. Instinctively, he moved sideways from it, and felt something brush briefly up against his side as if it were being pushed by the other shadow that had moved with it from the aforementioned darkness.

Aaron actually shook for a time with sheer fear. He knelt there, making himself as small and compact as possible. Abruptly, he stretched out a tired leg, and as he looked up toward the far wall, the shadowy black, half-materialized hand seemed to be rising up from the shadows, and appeared to move almost against his face before stopping when another more sedate looking feminine shadow hand seemed to grasp it and restrain it from proceeding any further.

Apart from the dazed fright, Aaron had for a moment a spiritual arousal, as if some delicate, beautiful, inward grace had stayed the danger that was overwhelming him. The whispering continued, and it was as if the evil one was being tormented and stymied in its pursuit of Aaron's total destruction. As the whispering died down, the cold breeze swept in again.

Something ghastly in the dark began to moan again, and the air became so heavy that it seemed to actually be enveloping Aaron, squeezing him with a cold embrace as the horrible breeze with a smell of decay blew upon him from behind the bed.

He quietly faced the corner from which the wind blew. A queer knowledge came that something was near him; yet nothing happened. Aaron sat in the chair surrounded by darkness, and he heard the whispering sound, then the moan.

The slight, smelly breeze blew steadily. To Aaron's astonishment, it quickly changed directions, seeming to come from behind him, and Aaron whipped around, with a hideous quake of fear. The breeze appeared to slap him in the face. It suddenly began to blow up from the floor in a quivering manner and the hideous, deathly, decaying smell penetrated Aaron's nostrils, almost making him regurgitate. Was the devil arising from the depths of hell to claim Hopkins House?

Suddenly, bewildered and confused, Aaron was aware that there was something in the far corner near the bed. A shadowy outline convulsed and vibrated as an unearthly, whining, low moan emanated from the shadow. The moan was so pitiful that it penetrated to the very depths of Aaron's soul. The thing was in agony, seemingly crying out for release from a torment of indescribable hell.

Other, more sinister looking shadows began to take shape all about the room. The one convoluting shadow that was moaning seemed to be pleading with the other four shadows that were gradually materializing. Yes, there were now five shadows. Four of them seemed to be of more sinister intent. They were apparent in their evil manifestations, and the smell. The evil, putrid smell of decaying flesh overwhelmed Aaron and finally he heaved up vomit that spilled onto the floor.

Raising his gun, he was determined to stop this terror by the sound of bullets exploding, but just as his trigger finger wrapped firmly about the trigger; an invisible thing jerked the gun from his hand with incredible and brutal force, flinging it against the far wall. A great, black shadow was beside him now, and rose into the air. Above that shadow, a dark shadow in the form of a hand was raised from the sinewy form. The hand plunged downward toward Aaron. Then, the shadow that had been moaning piteously, like a bolt of lighting moved in front of Aaron and the hand was stayed in mid air. Did Aaron have a protector among these shadowy demons of darkness?

Immediately conscious of a queer prickling sensation about the back of his head, Aaron's hands began to sweat profusely. The following instant, he turned and the whole wall where the spot was, flicked a crimson colour. There came a succeeding deep darkness that started in one corner of the wall and moved gradually to the other corner.

As he stooped forward, staring at the center of the room and listening, there came a crashing thud from the middle of the room. The sound echoed hollowly all about Aaron. And then the infernal knocking from hell started, thud, thud, thud, followed by a silence that was almost worse than the noise; an eerie, deathly, penetrating silence that crashed like a giant wave on the shore of a deserted, lonely beach.

Aaron had the feeling that something awful was stealing upon him from behind. Aaron stared straight ahead; too fearful to turn and face whatever he knew was moving toward him. There was something in the darkness behind him that was moving precipitously toward his back. He could sense it as the hair on the back of his neck prickled.

He had an abrupt, extraordinary sense of weirdness thrust upon him, as it were, a sense of something inhuman approaching from behind that was intending him grievous harm.

The midnight clock has tolled; and hark, the bell
Of death beats slow, heard ye the note profound?
It pauses now; and now, with rising knell,
Flings to the hallow gale its sullen sound.

Mason

Aaron felt death approaching from behind. Yet, he could not turn out of fear that what he would see was of such horror that his mind would snap. The smell, the smell of death and decay was so overwhelming that he thought he would faint, as it penetrated his nostrils and traveled upward toward his brain. Death was at hand. He looked to the floor and saw a huge shadow of a being hovering above him in a menacing fashion. Just as he prepared to dash for the door, another shadow of what appeared to be a woman, approached from the side with extended hand, in what appeared to be a signal to halt, to cease this evil manifestation and return to the pit of darkness from which the shadow came.

Suddenly the sweet smell of lilacs replaced the horrible odour of death, and the cold breeze ceased. As Aaron turned to see what was behind him, he saw the menacing shadow dissipate and a shadow of a woman near the spot on the wall. A woman's voice whispered softly, "Go from this devil's den of inequity. The evil ones are stayed for now."

At the last word, the woman's shadow diminished in size. Aaron turned and gingerly made his way toward the door. The dawn came slowly through the windows and he could see no signs of anything or anyone in the room. Walking through the doorway, and closing the door behind him, he left the terror of the night behind him. He went into all the third floor rooms, then the second floor as well. He was searching for Rachael. Surely, her night had been filled with the horrible sounds emanating from that vile room where he had come face-to-face with unmitigated, unchained, abhorrent evil.

Leaving the terror of the night behind, he went to the first floor to continue his search, to no avail. Looking at the front door, he noticed that it was unlocked, so he assumed Rachael had probably left to get something to fix for breakfast.

He could not wait for her. There were things he needed to do. He found a tablet and wrote her a short note saying that he would be back around sunset, and he would have definitive information on the locket, because he now was sure he knew where it might be. Last night, in the dark, he had remembered something that would lead him to it.

As he left the house, he could not help but look over his shoulder and think about what he had experienced there. The evil that plagued Hopkins House was a secondary consideration for him now. First and foremost was the love that had developed between him and Rachael. She had changed his life, and he expected that he, too, had changed hers. Together, they would be a formidable pair who would overcome any obstacle presented by Hopkins House.

Aaron's first stop was his office, where he shaved, showered and changed clothes, except for his underwear. He could not help but laugh when he looked into his spare clothes drawer and saw that there was no clean underwear. It reminded him of his beloved grandmother, who taught him at an early age that when you are short of underwear, you just turn it inside out and wear it another day. That was one of many things she had taught him, but there was one more thing that he had forgotten for a long time.

During the fearful night in Hopkins House, he remembered that his grandmother, when he was a young boy, had discussed a man named Mark Hopkins with him. He was a man she was extremely familiar with through stories she had heard from her mother over the years. Aaron realized that by finding out more about Mark Hopkins, he might also find out more about Harry

Hopkins, who might just be related. Although they were years apart in age, there might be a thread that would link them to this perplexing mystery. Aaron stopped at the Manhattan Public Library and looked up Mark Hopkins in the card catalogue. The connection between Mark Hopkins and the Harry Hopkins family might lead him to the story behind the locket, and maybe to the locket itself. Unfortunately, there were two Mark Hopkins. One was from New York, and the other one from North Carolina. The two wound up in San Francisco at the same time. The story of the North Carolina Mark Hopkins was most interesting. He and his brother Moses left for Kentucky after stealing horses in Randolph County, North Carolina in the early 1850's. Eventually, they wound up in California. There were conflicting stories about which Mark Hopkins helped build a railroad through the Sierra Nevada Mountains and became one of America's richest men. So rich, that he built a magnificent Victorian home atop San Francisco's famous Nob Hill.

Then the story took a faithful turn when Aaron read further. In 1906, the house was destroyed in the San Francisco earthquake. Today, on the very spot where the house stood, is the world famous Mark Hopkins Hotel. He further found that Mark Hopkins, Jr. (the son of Mark Hopkins) and Harry Hopkins were both in San Francisco in 1906, and so was the locket.

Spending hours poring over dusty books, magazines and newspapers, Aaron came upon a picture in a 1906 San Francisco Examiner that not only connected Harry and Mark Hopkins' son (Mark Hopkins, Jr.), but someone else who was germane to the mysterious locket. In the newspaper was an article about Harry Hopkins joining his cousin Mark, Jr. in San Francisco, where Harry had opened a clothing factory. With them in a photograph was a third person, the recent widow of a man who had sold the property for a new factory to Harry Hopkins. This woman was wearing a cameo locket around her neck, and the caption said she was Mrs. Andrew R. Bandini.

Immediately, Aaron knew that she had to be a relative of Arturo Bandini. Yes, Arturo Bandini knew more about the locket than he was telling. The woman in the photo was wearing the locket. That crafty old man was concealing information that might lead Aaron to the locket. Aaron's next stop would be the Bandini home.

Greeted at the door by Arturo's grandson who was dressed in high heels, a red mini-skirt and a tight fitting blouse that was accentuated by the breast forms with perky nipples, Aaron could not help but think the young transvestite did, indeed, make a beautiful woman.

"Mr. Adams, how nice it is to see you again. My great grandfather is out right now, but he will be back around 6:00 P.M., I think. I am on my way out for an early dinner; would you like to join me? Or, would you be ashamed to be seen with me?"

Aaron had nothing else to do, and he was non-judgemental enough not to care who saw him with the young Bandini. After all, most of the finger-pointers were worse than the ones they were pointing fingers at, anyway.

"No, I will join you. Why should I be ashamed to be seen with you?" Aaron said as he stepped to the side and waited for Bandini to join him on the stoop.

Smiling, a delighted Bandini took Aaron's arm as he offered it, and they walked down the stairs, turned right and headed up the street.

Bandini was obviously shocked by Aaron's lack of concern about being seen with a transvestite and said, "You are a strange man, Mr. Adams. Usually a virile looking manly-man like you is a bit self-conscious about being seen with someone like me. I am used to finger-pointing and ridicule from people everywhere

I go. I am afraid I have been ostracized by a great many people over the past ten years as I began to realize I was a woman in a man's body."

Aaron, smiling broadly replied, "Well, you do not have a body like any man I ever knew."

Giggling at the compliment, Bandini replied, "You certainly know how to make a girl feel good."

"Thank you. I did not realize you were a transsexual rather than a transvestite. I apologize, because I do know the difference."

"No need to apologize, Mr. Adams, as most people do not know the difference. I, fortunately, have a dear great grandfather who does, and in three months we have scheduled the surgery that will change me to what I should have been. I am fortunate in having a family member who will stand by me as I correct this horrible mistake of nature."

As they entered Luigi's Restaurant, Aaron noticed the glaring eyes of the patrons, but made sure he treated Bandini like a lady, removing her jacket and pulling out the seat for her. Sitting across from her, looking directly in her eyes, Aaron said, "You are lucky to have a great grandfather wise enough to know you have no control over your condition. He is a wonderful, understanding man."

"You are so right, and I think you are, too, Mr. Adams."

Aaron, obviously thankful for the compliment replied, "I try to be, but I am afraid I often fall short, especially when lied to by people I trust. For example, I am having trouble accepting your great grandfather's story about the locket and what happened when your grandfather returned from school after his mother's death. Would you know anything about it at all?"

"Well, I know about the locket, and I do know that my great grandfather lied to you for your own good. He feared for your life. There is a long and sordid history of how that locket has for decades bound the Bandini and Hopkins families. Many in both families considered it the source of despair for two families doomed by association with that evil piece of the devil's jewellery."

Aaron leaning forward asked, "Can you tell me more?"

"I am afraid I am not the one with the depth of knowledge you seek, but I do know that my great grandfather can explain it all. When my grandfather left for Cuba to fight for justice, he received assurance from my dear, departed grandmother that the locket would be safely stored where no one could find it. Only she and my great grandfather knew its whereabouts. She died a few years ago in her bedroom, late at night. The coroner said she died of unknown causes, but my great grandfather is sure she died of fright. She had a horrible look of fear on her face when we found her, and there was a slight burn on her left cheek. That day, she and my great grandfather had checked for the first time in years to see that the locket was still securely locked away from prying eyes. I suggest we finish our dinner, and that you see my great grandfather for clarification. I am sure he will be willing to offer you all the information you seek when I tell him how gallant and gracious you have been to me."

Finishing their dinner, the two enjoyed each other's company a while longer as they had one last drink. Aaron paid the check, and the whole place was aghast as Aaron pulled out her chair and helped her on with her jacket. The damning stares were just an example of people's ignorance thought Aaron.

Offering her his arm, they meandered out of the place, heads held high in defiance of a tradition bound, hypocritical culture that tried to make everyone conform to predetermined roles. Tradition be damned, Aaron was a man who would defy the sameness that made America a land of sanctimonious, judgemental, fascist finger-pointers.

As they walked down the street, Aaron could see that his new found friend took great pride in being on his arm, unashamed and defiant with her head held high. He thought how horrible that good people had to live their lives in the shadows in order to avoid condemnation in a society ruled by judgmental bigots who controlled and manipulated the poor mindless sheep that were too wrapped up in religious dogma and patriotic babble to think for themselves.

It gave Aaron great solace and a warm feeling of accomplishment to know that he had, in a small way, helped give Bandini some self-respect and pride. Where were the Christians when people like Bandini cried out for compassion and understanding? They were usually in their expensive church pews, pointing the fingers of condemnation, rather than embracing people like Bandini with love and understanding, as their beloved Jesus would have done.

Aaron thought about the arrogant evangelists on television who declare that God does not make mistakes. Hell, the TV evangelists were the biggest mistakes of all. God allowing them to pontificate and institutionalize hate as an integral part of so-called Christianity was an affront to human decency. Letting Hitler be born was not a mistake? According to some Christians, of course not, because he gassed the Jews, who for centuries had been the targets of hatred, preached by the Christian church. Letting children be born to the poor, so they could die of starvation was not a mistake? Letting America develop a bomb that could kill hundreds of thousands of Orientals in Hiroshima and Nagasaki was not a mistake, because those killed were not Christians? Putting a dunce like Ronald Reagan in office was not a mistake, because the wealthy needed better representation and the poor were getting too much welfare, anyway? God make mistakes, why of course he didn't.

As they continued down the street, Aaron sensed that Bandini was a genuinely kind and caring person. Some day, perhaps the U.S.A. might be a place where people like her could be accepted, but he harboured little hope of it happening in an America where the right-wing was in firm control and was rapidly turning the country into a theocracy that would one-day morph into a state where someone even more moronic than Reagan would open the gates of power to the purveyors of hate and judgmental arrogance in a way that would destroy what little decency there was left in the world's most corrupt, self-serving and arrogant society.

Walking up the stoop, Bandini turned to Aaron and said, "You have been very nice to me Aaron. I hope you will become my friend. I am afraid I have few."

"Well, I would love to be your friend, and I am sure a nice girl like you will have many friends as you grow older and mature into a woman. By the way, I do not know your name. I hate to just call you Miss Bandini."

Obviously grateful that Aaron accepted her as a woman, she replied, "My original name was Randy, which is appropriate for a woman too, don't you think?"

"Yes, it is Randy. I once knew a girl in grade school named Randy."

Randy was beaming with joy as she basked in the glorious acceptance and approval Aaron offered her. Opening the door, she was impressed with Aaron's politeness as he waited for her to enter first. As they went down the hall, she called out for her great grandfather, and he told her to come into the study.

"Grand One, look who is with me."

"Mr. Adams, how nice to see you again."

"You may not be so happy to see him when you know why he is here my dear," said Randy as she winked at Aaron.

"Randy is right, Mr. Bandini. I am afraid that I know you have been keeping something from me, something that is very important to my client."

Randy knew that her presence might serve as an impediment to her great grandfather freely discussing matters with Aaron, so she said, "It is nearly 7 o'clock, and I do have a date for dancing at 8. I am sure you two gentleman will excuse a lady who needs to shower and change clothes so she can do some hoofing tonight."

Both men smiled and nodded their heads in acquiescence. Randy left the room, and Aaron felt that she was going to make it in a world that made it difficult for her. She had that something that was indiscernible, but it was there, a certain oomph that made you see she would be alright, no matter what the world threw at her.

A brief interlude of small talk as the two men heard the shower running upstairs was broken with a directness that did not seem to suit Mr. Bandini. "Well, Mr. Adams, I know what you are here for tonight, but I hope you will understand the consternation I had and still have in regards to that infernal thing that has plagued the lives of two families for far too long, now."

"I do understand, sir. I sincerely do, but I have a mission that cannot be fulfilled without your help. I hope that you will afford me the courtesy of your trust in doing the right thing. Believe me, although I may not always succeed, I try very hard to be a man of honour. I would do nothing to intentionally harm you, Randy or anyone in the Hopkins family. I know how much you have all suffered over the years. I sincerely want to bring an end to this horror."

Scratching his bald pate, Mr. Bandini in a sincere voice said, "For many years Mr. Adams, I have genuinely felt that I was the keeper of the key that kept the gates of hell locked. I think you are due an explanation, and with your indulgence, I will provide you with one, so that perhaps you can bring some peace and solace to both families. I must first share with you the agony of someone who lost the dearest person in his life to the ghosts that you think are so prevalent now in Hopkins House. Believe me; the terror is much more perverse than the mere haunting of Hopkins House. The ancient Japanese curse of *Ju On* does not only exist in Japan. It is here, in America, too. You see, that infernal locket comes from Japan, and I firmly believe that there is a demon connected with it. I assumed that I had locked the demon up for all time, but if what you tell me of Hopkins House is true, I have never had the demon confined. I have lived under an illusion all these years. I do believe that there is something inherently vile that I have been able to confine by locking that thing up, but I also know that the real evil is loose; it is loose in Hopkins House and has been for almost sixty years. I feel personally responsible for much of what happened, because I now know that the locket should have been returned to Hopkins House long ago. I sincerely believe that the only way to stay the evil is by returning that locket to that house, but before doing so, you must know more of its history and how it has promulgated evil for so long."

He got up, went to the bookshelf and removed an ancient looking book. He opened it and took out a folded small piece of paper. "Mr. Adams, my wife was a haunted woman, just as the Hopkins family is haunted. I never shared this with anyone after her death, because I feared that someone might think she had died by her own hand. You see, I found it among her things in an old jewellery case. You should know that it was dated the day before she died."

Opening the small paper, he handed it to Aaron. Written on it was a poem:

THE HORRORS OF SLEEP

Sleep brings me no joy.
Remembrance never dies,
My soul is given to mystery,
And lives in sighs.

Sleep brings no rest to me;
The shadows of the dead
My wakening eyes may never see
Surround my bed.

Sleep brings no hope to me,
In soundest sleep they come,
And with their doleful imagery
Deepen the gloom.

Sleep brings no strength to me,
No power renewed to brave;
I only sail a wilder sea,
A darker wave.

Sleep brings no friend to me
To sooth and aid to bear;
They all gaze on, how scornfully,
And I despair.

Sleep brings no wish to fret
My harassed heart beneath;
My only wish to forget
In endless sleep of death.

  Surprised, Aaron said, "So, your wife was haunted by the same evil that is prevalent in Hopkins House. Are you telling me that the power of *Ju On* can escape the confines of a home?"

"That is exactly what I am telling you, Mr. Adams."

"This evil knows no boundaries when it comes to the Bandini and Hopkins families. I am overwhelmed by the battle I have fought against this all these years, and understand how the Hopkins clan has also been locked in a struggle with this evil."

"Mr. Adams, I was surprised when you informed me you were hired by someone who wanted to rid the Hopkins House of this evil, for I assumed that there were no members of the Hopkins family left. I know that the house was rented many times by an estate agent over the years, but that all the tenants only lasted a short time before violently dying or being driven from there by some perverted, unidentifiable evil. Most of the time, the house just sat there empty, casting a dark pale over Farragut Street that bathed the area in the darkness of its pervasive evil."

Aaron knew that he must learn how this evil came about, how the whole sordid mess actually started, and he felt Arturo Bandini was now eager to tell him the entire story. "Mr. Bandini, I need to know all that occurred that led to this evil, so that I can properly attack it and finally bring an end to this heinous misery."

Arturo took a deep breath and began the story. "My uncle, Andrew Bandini, who was a bit of a rogue and a rapscallion, went west in the 1850's. While there, around 1900, he married a young woman 40 years his junior, and there was very little love from her for him. It appears that she had plenty of love for a variety of men, but not my uncle. Yet, he was immensely enamoured with her, and refused to countenance any hint of ending the marriage. He simply put up with her infidelities and counted himself lucky to have such a beautiful woman in his presence on a regular basis."

"My uncle met a man named Leland Stanford, Jr. They became great friends, and may have even had some business dealings together. I am sure you recognize the name as his father is the benefactor of a prestigious, well-known university which bears his name, Stanford University. Anyway, Leland Stanford, Jr. was also in business with Mark Hopkins, Jr., as they were bankrolled by their incredibly wealthy fathers who had started, along with a man named Huntington, the Central Pacific Railroad that went through the Sierra Nevada Mountain gold fields."

"Leland Stanford, Jr. introduced my uncle to Mark Hopkins, Jr. That was the beginning of the terror. Becoming good friends, my uncle and Mark Hopkins, Jr. were often together, and there was one day when they were meandering about the shop district near Nob Hill, just browsing for some expensive baubles to give to their young and materially impressionable young wives, whom they tried to keep satisfied through the attainment of possessions that the women felt were the measure of worth."

"As the story has been told and retold over the years, and no doubt, been embellished a bit in the process, an old, decrepit woman mysteriously appeared before Mark Hopkins, Jr. and Andrew Bandini one day when the two men were in a curio shop, looking for gifts for their wives. She said that she had the perfect gift for one of their wives. She showed them a Japanese cameo locket that she claimed was cursed, as it had been in a home where violent murders were committed in the late 1700's. These murders had led to a *Ju On* curse, which traps those who are part of evil acts within the confines of the place where those acts were committed. The woman said she had come into possession of the locket when the house burned to the ground after someone mysteriously opened the locket, and, according to the woman, ended the curse by trapping a demon within. She gave them strict instructions to never open the locket. It was to only be admired for its outward beauty. Of course, both men scoffed at the admonition, as being arrogant westerners, they saw the Orientals as foolish, superstitious illiterates, and this old woman as nothing better. With the intention of deciding who should have it at a later time, the two men paid the old woman, looked down to admire the cameo and the beautiful box in which it was placed. When they looked up again, the old woman had disappeared."

"Deciding who should have it was an easy task for the two gamblers. A toss of a coin made my uncle think he had won, when in reality, in this case, the loser was the ultimate winner."

Aaron was warming to the story. He licked his lips and leaned forward, waiting for the next instalment of the intriguing tale.

"My uncle made a gift of the cameo to his young wife. A few weeks later, Mark Hopkins, Jr. introduced my uncle to Harry Hopkins who was searching for some land on which to build a factory, as he had come west to exploit cheap Oriental labour. Andrew Bandini made the deal with Harry Hopkins, but a few weeks later, Andrew Bandini met his death outside his Nob Hill mansion. He was found on his front door step with a hatchet buried in his back. The hatchet came from the gardener's shed behind the mansion. It was his wife who found him and called the police. Harriet Bandini came under suspicion, but she was never charged."

Aaron asked, "Why did they suspect her?"

"She was the only one home at the time of the murder. She also, along with the gardener, was the only one with a key to the storage shed. The lock had not been broken, and the shed was still locked when the body was found. The gardener was on vacation and was out of the city when the murder occurred. The hatchet was clearly marked with an *AB*, which, according to the gardener, was the hatchet from the shed."

Bandini wiped his eyes and squinted. He reached into his desk and removed a small flask, took a drink from it and gestured toward Aaron to see if he wanted a swig.

Aaron indicated that he was fine, and Arturo continued his story. "This is where the story takes one of many bizarre turns. Exactly four months to the day after Andrew Bandini's death, his wife, Harriet, committed suicide by falling on a butcher knife in the kitchen. On a countertop, the police found the cameo. It was not considered evidence, as Harriet had obviously committed suicide due to grief or remorse in regards to my uncle's death, so it languished in the house, until an auction was held. According to witnesses, it was bought by a decrepit, old woman."

Aaron interjected, "And the cameo locket wound up in the same curio shop where it was bought by Candace Hopkins. Am I right?"

"Yes, Mr. Adams, the locket was destined to be an instrument of terror for both the Bandini and Hopkins families. You see, it was brought back from San Francisco to Manhattan, and you know that it was in the Hopkins' household for a long time, until it wound up at the Salvation Army Thrift Store. I know you are aware of how the infernal thing wound up back within the Bandini clan. It is a propitiously sinister occurrence that the two families keep coming into possession of the locket."

Aaron sensed that the old man was growing despondent as he poured forth with the story of misery and woe wrought on two families that were trapped in a decade's long downward spiral into a deep, gloomy abyss of darkness. Almost apologetically, Aaron asked, "You were arguing with Candace about the locket, because you feared the evil would be unleashed if she had it."

"Yes, I had suffered the death of my beloved wife. I had seen my less beloved sister-in-law, whom I abhorred, but would have never wished dead, die by stabbing herself with a butcher knife. I simply refused to give Candace Hopkins the locket, and I demanded that she stop using my son as a pawn to retrieve that monstrous, evil bauble of abomination."

Aaron thought in abject silence. Should he tell Bandini the truth as relayed by Rachael to him? Yes, he thought, yes, the old man was entitled to the truth. "Mr. Bandini, Candace wanted the locket for the same reason I do. She thought the evil could only be contained inside the cameo. Once the locket was opened, the evil was free within Hopkins House. The only way to contain it is to open the locket, so the evil can return there, and the locket can be closed to confine it. That was her mission. It is a mission my client can only complete for Candace, if you allow me to return the locket to Hopkins House. My client is convinced that it is the only way to stay the evil presence that has manifested itself for nearly sixty years there. Frankly, I am still sceptical about the whole thing, but I know she believes this is the only way to end the evil that plagues Hopkins House."

Just as Arturo was about to respond, Randy Bandini popped her head through the archway and said, "Goodbye gentleman. This girl is going out for some fun."

Arturo told her to have a good time. Aaron smiled and nodded his approval. Before leaving Randy thanked Aaron for a wonderful time, turned and gave him a nice glimpse of a curvaceously shaped ass as she waved good bye.

Arturo Bandini returned to the subject at hand and said in a pensive manner, "I must give you the locket, Mr. Adams. However, you must promise me that once this evil menace is contained, you will see to it that the locket is protected from ever being opened again. You must see to it that no other families fall victim to this evil curse that has claimed so many in the Bandini and Hopkins families."

"You have my word that I will assiduously see to it that the locket is properly taken care of once my client has used it to stop the evil manifestations she assumes are plaguing Hopkins House."

Arturo got up and motioned for Aaron to follow him. They went through the kitchen and down into the wine cellar. Moving through the wine racks, which had obviously gone unused for years, Arturo went to a small rack hidden away in the corner. He removed a bottle of Merlot and placed it on an adjacent table. The label was dated 1925. He picked up a cork screw and said, "a waste of good wine I am afraid, Mr. Adams."

Aaron could not figure out what Arturo was doing. What did a bottle of wine have to do with the locket?

Smiling, the old man poured the contents into a bucket on the floor until it was almost empty. Then Aaron saw it, a small container slithered through the neck of the bottle onto Arturo's palm. The air tight container was placed on the table and Arturo said, "Open it."

Aaron tried, but could not open the container. Again smiling, Arturo walked over to a small work table. He placed the container in a vice and picked up a pair of pliers. With the container wedged in the vice, he placed the pliers on the top part of the container, pulled and the top popped off. There it was. There, no bigger than a thumbnail was the tiny cameo locket.

Arturo made a sweeping motion with his right hand, indicating it was Aaron's to take. Aaron picked it up, examined it, and could not fully comprehend how this tiny thing could possibly be the root of so much evil. Yet, after a night in Hopkins House, he was willing to admit there were things he simply could not explain.

Was Aaron finally coming to the end of this journey into darkness? Could this be the final piece of the puzzle that would assuage Rachael's fears, and allow Aaron and her to put all this behind them? Could they finally leave that infernal house together and walk out of the darkness and despair into the harmony and peace he longed for with her?

Aaron put the locket in his right side coat pocket and the two men proceeded upstairs. They stopped for a moment in the kitchen and Arturo, with a strange look on his face, a look of impending doom, said, "Go into the study Mr. Adams, I have something else to show you, but first, I must get a glass of water. May I get you anything?"

"No, I am fine," said Aaron as he turned and went down the hallway into the study. He had a seat and while waiting, he thought about how much simpatico he had with Arturo. He had really grown to admire the man after a couple of brief visits. He was impressed with his humanity and concern for those who were forgotten by a society mired in greed and religious dogma. Here was a man who still harboured a deep-rooted passion for social justice in a country that trampled on it like it was an infectious disease.

Aaron saw an old book of poems that had been laid out on the desk. He picked it up, sat back down, started reading a poem about death and wondered what was taking Arturo so long. He heard a strange gurgling noise coming from down the hallway, near the kitchen. He could not wait much longer as he needed to see Rachael by dusk. He got up and slowly walked down the hallway, intently listening to the unusual gurgling noise that penetrated the deathly quietness of the house.

At the kitchen entrance, Aaron froze in his tracts, standing there, staring straight ahead and remembering the poem.

The Darkness

While some affect the sun, we all eventually find shade.
With different aims, various roads we take,
But all destined for the gloomy horrors of the tomb.
It is the place of rendezvous, where all
Life's travelers will ultimately meet.
To be evaluated at the great judgment seat.

There is the eternal King, whose potent arms sustain
The keys of death, heaven and hell.
The Grave, oh the grave, dreadful thing.
Men shiver when it is named.
Yet, death will not be denied
In the place where darkness and silence reigns.

Let fall the supernumerary horror,
Which serves to make fear of darkness irksome.
See those with earthly fame - pious work -
Recognized names now dubious or forgot.
And buried midst the wreck of things that were;
There lie interred the great illustrious dead.

The wind is up, and how it howls.
Until now, never heard a sound so dreary:
Thinking back on Hopkins House,
Doors creak, windows clap, gloom abides.
Wrapped in screams of anguish,
Mansion of the dead, roused from their slumbers.

In grim array the spectres will rise,
Moan horrible and obstinately sullen,
Pass and re-pass, hushed as the foot of ghosts.
It makes one's blood chill,
To think of those who go quiet
Into the silent and dark of night.

Wild shrieks have echoed from hollow tombs.
The dead will come again and walk about.
The dead who lie below
Tell naught in homely phrase
As apparitions tall and ghastly,
Walk at the dead of night.

Then, those of us left to grieve
Are such a sorrowful, pitiful sight.

Slow moving, the living over the prostrate dead,
Listless, they crawl along in doleful black,
While bursts of sorrow gush from either eye,
Fast falling down swollen, sunken cheek.

Prone on the lowly grave of the dear ones loved,
We drop while busy meddling memory,
In barbarous succession, muster up
The past endearments softer hours
Tenacious of its theme. Oh, insidious grave.
Those who struggled in a thing called life
Are now dead, but how we must wonder
Do they lie in peace,
Or are things still asunder?

Stunned, Aaron slowly regained his composure. What he observed had momentarily put him in a near trance state. His blood was still running cold, and the noise, the infernal gurgling noise seemed to pound in his head. The insides of his stomach rushed upward, and he caught the vomit half-way up his throat. Why did this have to happen to Arturo Bandini?

Arturo was in a sitting position, leaning over, actually propped up on a butcher knife that was imbedded deeply into his chest. The wound was making horrible gurgling noises as the blood oozed onto the floor.

Aaron knew there was nothing he could do for him. He patted his right coat pocket and felt for the locket. There seemed to be warmth on the jacket material. Why would just the area where the locket was be warm? He also, instinctively, patted his left breast to make sure that the 45 was still holstered and ready to serve. False security he thought. He looked one last time at Arturo Bandini, and hoped that his misery was over. He hoped it was time to also end the misery for Rachael. It was time to put the ghosts of Hopkins House to rest.

EPILOGUE
RACHAEL

For a long time, Aaron just stood there on the stoop of Hopkins House. The darkness was creeping over it. No, it seemed to be embracing it. There was evil there like Aaron had never known before. He had seen evil in many forms in his life. He had experienced the raw human emotions of watching his comrades die agonizing deaths as a result of the evil promulgated by uncaring politicians who sent the poor off to fight wars of conquest. He had seen the evil of a society based on greed. He had seen the evil of avaricious living by the wealthy and powerful who eschewed any semblance of decency in response to the needs of their fellow citizens. He had seen the evil of injustice as the poor were demonized for their plight. Yet, the evil of Hopkins House was different, but by no means worse than the other evils of a corrupt society in the land of indifference. The vast array of power promulgated by the rich and powerful made it almost impossible, short of a genuine revolution, to stay the evil of the corrupt American system of capitalism, but the evil of Hopkins House was about to be washed away by the sunshine of love Aaron had for Rachael. The end of the terror was at hand. Still, as Aaron continued to stare at the gloomy mansion, uneasiness came over him. The evil was waiting within, and he sensed it was ready to do battle to keep its hold on Hopkins House.

Staring at the upper floor stairwell window, Aaron caught a glimpse of what appeared to be a dark figure moving about. He moved about two steps down, and looked straight up. The whole street seemed to be getting darker. He noticed that none of the street lights were on. Yet, beyond Farragut, he could see the lights brightly glowing. The moon cast an eerie glow on the upper floor stairwell window. Aaron saw the dark shadow seemingly moving about the landing. He went into a trance like state again just as he had done at Arturo Bandini's earlier in the evening. His thoughts were of Rachael and Hopkins House.

Ghost House

Rachael dwells in a lonely house I know.
Its people vanished many a summer ago.
And left no trace but the evil walls,
And a Ju-On curse as the night falls
In a place where incredibly wild stories grow.
Over ruins of sanity, the evil shields
The ghosts who come back to the haunting fields.
On the stoop where many stand,
The footpath to evil never healed.
Evil dwells with a strangely aching heart
In the vanished glory there far apart
On the ghostly road fed,
The ultimate evil was wed.
Night comes, the blackness abides.
The lonely owl is coming to shout,
Hush, cluck and flutter about.
You can hear evil begin slightly far away
And full many a time have its say.
Evil is under a dim, dark star.
You can only sense who these ghostly folk are,
Grudgingly sharing the place with mortal intruders.
They are tireless ghosts evil and sad.
Be careful not to make them mad.
None among them ever sings
Of any happy things.
Be aware that those who dare to tread
Among those who are long dead
May find themselves like the intrepid liar
Trapped with a demon in eternal fire.

Snapping back out of his Frost-induced trance, Aaron noticed the curtain in the stairwell had been drawn. The house was in complete darkness. He assumed Rachael might not be in, but he moved up the stoop and pulled the bell vociferously, and eventually heard the patter of feet moving toward the door.

There she was in all her radiant beauty. It was if the door had opened into sublime paradise. She smiled provocatively and flung herself into Aaron's arms. The emotion of the moment made Aaron forget for awhile why he was there. Feeling Rachael in his arms made his blood race through his veins like a river through a gorge. He reached down and held both her hands, just staring into her eyes. As always her hands were extremely cold, but she had already proven that she had a warm heart. Leading her into the parlour, he motioned for her to have a seat beside him.

Sitting on the sofa, placing his right hand on her lap, Aaron said, "My dear, I have the news for which you have waited so long. I have the locket."

"I knew that you would not fail me my sweet. I never doubted that you would help me end this terror."

Slightly hesitating, Aaron reached in his pocket and removed the locket. Handing it to her he said, "What is the next step, Rachael?"

"Aaron, I am so grateful for your help. I know that you will not understand a lot of what must now occur, but please bear with me, and trust me to do what I must in order to finish the work you have done. It is only I who can now complete the circle that will finally bring an end to a terror that has walked these halls for nearly sixty years."

Placing the locket on the coffee table, Rachael continued, "I have not left this house in many years. That is why the notes were delivered to your office by a messenger. I have lived in darkness for too long now. I have been a prisoner of the night, but you have made it possible for the entire Hopkins family to be free – truly free of this abominable curse which has made the family slaves to the demon that brought this evil to Hopkins House."

Reaching out and hugging Aaron, she pulled him to her, holding him in a loving embrace. There were a few seconds of silence as Aaron felt something seem to go out of him. A deep emotional bond had developed between the two lovers, and now Aaron felt that bond even more. From the very core of his inner being, he knew that Rachael felt the same. They were eternally bound together now.

Loosening her grip on Aaron, Rachael looked deep into his eyes and said, "I know one day you will understand why I must do what I am about to do, alone. You have experienced the horrors of that abominable room. Believe me; I have no fear of what those creatures can do to me. I am beyond the pale of their cruelty and evil machinations. And now, with the locket, I am a formidable beacon of light in the darkness that engulfs Hopkins House. However, you must promise me that after tonight, after this house is finally rid of evil incarnate, the locket will be put where it can never again be opened and the evil unleashed on the unsuspecting. I leave it to you to decide where it must go. I suggest the deepest river, the highest mountain or the hottest fire, so that others may be spared the evil that it breeds."

Aaron assured her that he knew a steel worker who would put it in a coke oven and melt it into oblivion, and that he would stand there until every last molecule was dissolved in a fire that was as hot as hell itself.

Smiling, Rachael got up, stood before Aaron, picked up the locket, rolled it in her palm and said, "Please wait for fifteen minutes dearest Aaron. I will be in that room only a short while. Then, you may come in, and everything will be clear. Remember that I depend on you to see that once the locket is closed for the last time in that room, it will never again be opened under any circumstances. I want you to know that I love you as I have never loved another man. You are life itself to me."

Alarmed at the finality of her tone, Aaron addressed her in a stern infliction, "You seem as if you do not expect to see me again."

"Far from it my dear, I expect to see you every single day that you live, and then to spend a blissful eternity with you."

"Rachael what are you going to do in that room?"

Rachael turned, slowly walked to the archway that led into the hall and as she left said, "Sweet Aaron, I am going to do what I must. You will understand one day that there is no other way."

Aaron forlornly watched her walk down the hall and move slowly up the stairs, but there was no trepidation in her gait. She had a determined countenance to her bearing with shoulders pulled back and head held high. In silence Aaron lost sight of her as he could not see beyond the second floor landing. He was resigned to doing as she asked.

Thinking over the events of the past few days, he knew that he must not lose her. He could not give up the woman who in only a matter of days had become his whole life.

Heading back to the parlour, Aaron had a seat and looked longingly at the floor, remembering that he and Rachael had made passionate love there. Then, he looked over at the sofa arm and recollected the magnificent way he had mounted her from behind. Amidst all this turmoil, Aaron looked down at his trousers, noticing that he had an erection.

He noticed the old photo of Rachael had been placed on the fireplace mantel. He got up, strolled over, picked up the frame and stood there admiring the old photo of a girl who had grown into a woman, a woman with whom he was deeply in love. He looked at the frame and studied the picture closely. Standing there, he was trying to figure out what was so odd about it.

He suddenly dropped the picture to the floor as he was frightened by a loud scream coming from that horrid room. He did not care what he promised Rachael. He was going up to the room.

As he was ascending the stairs, he sensed that horrible smell of decay all about the house. Bounding up two steps at a time, arriving on the second floor landing, he paused for a few seconds as he heard the low, melodic moaning of several voices. The pain and the agony in those voices penetrated to the depths of Aaron's heart.

Unable to restrain himself any longer, he rapidly climbed the last flight of stairs and stood before the closed door of the room of pain. Suddenly the moaning ceased and a melodic happy tone seemed to bounce off the walls of the house. Then as he slowly opened the door, the decaying smell gave way to the scent of lilacs in full bloom.

Aaron surveyed the room. It was empty. He saw the closed locket lying on the corner dresser near where the infamous spot was. Only now, the spot was gone and the room seemed to be bathed in a soft, peaceful, bluish light.

He frantically called out for Rachael, but there was no response. Moving toward the dresser, he saw a piece of writing paper beneath the locket. Picking up the locket, he placed it in his pocket and then read the brief note.

Dearest Aaron, you have helped set the ghosts of the past free, and brought a serenity that transcends life and death to Hopkins House. I can not explain why I must go. But go I must. I shall love you for all time, but I encourage you to please not live in memories of me, for you deserve a life filled with happiness and love. It is the life I wish I could have lived with you. Love forever, Rachael.

Aaron could not figure out how she got out of the house without him noticing. After a thorough search of the residence, he finally gave up and went back to his office, secure in the knowledge that she would eventually turn up.

The next day, he took the locket to his friend who worked at City Steel and watched it burn in the coke oven. As it melted, finally dissipating into nothingness, he kept thinking of Rachael. Where was she? Why would she leave him?

Feeling morbid and despondent, some inner voice kept telling Aaron to stop by the public library and check out a book of Edgar Allen Poe's poetry. As a child, he had been particularly attracted to Poe, because his childhood was often melancholy. The poems of Poe were dispirited, sad and depressing. They were perfect for a child who by reading about death and misery sought solace in knowing that others shared his pain. Today, Aaron felt like that little boy again. His pain and anguish was overwhelming him. If only his beloved grandmother was still around for consolation. She had been his rock in a childhood of unmitigated turmoil.

Arriving at his office around 4:00 P.M., he took off his jacket and hung it on the rack by the sofa. He sat down, and lifted the jacket he had worn the previous day off the sofa arm and tossed it on the coffee table beside the Poe book, so he could lie his head on the sofa arm and stare at the ceiling for awhile. As he lay there, he reached over and picked up the book, opening it to the table of contents. There it was the third one down, *Annabel Lee*. That was the perfect poem for his mood. Many times, as a youth, when he had desperately loved a young girl, he had turned to that poem in his sorrow caused by rejection. One girl in particular, Carolyn Lassiter, had caught his fancy for many years, and eternal repudiation from her had made the young Aaron cuddle up many a night in bed to read *Annabel Lee* while contemplating his sorrowful state of mind, and how he might use another approach the following day to get her attention.

Aaron lifted the book above his face and read:

Annabel Lee

by

Edgar Allen Poe

It was many and many a year ago,
In a kingdom by the sea
That a maiden there lived whom you may know
By the name Annabel Lee;
And the maiden, she lived with no other thought
Than to love and be loved by me.

I was a child and she was a child,
In this kingdom by the sea;
But we loved with a love that was more than love –
I and my Annabel Lee –
With a love that weighed seraphs of heaven
Coveted her and me.

And this was the reason that, long ago,
In this kingdom by the sea,
A wind blew out of a cloud, chilling
My beautiful Annabel Lee;
So that her highborn kinsmen came
And bore her away from me,
To shut her up in a sepulchre
In this kingdom by the sea.

The angels, not half so happy in heaven,
Went envying her and me –
Yes! – that was the reason (as all men know,
In this kingdom by the sea)
That the wind came out of a cloud by night,
Chilling and killing my Annabel Lee.

But our love it was stronger by far than the love
Of those who were older than we –
Of many far wiser than we –
And neither the angels in heaven above,
Nor the demons down under the sea,
Can ever dissever my soul from the soul
Of the beautiful Annabel Lee.

For the moon never beams, without bringing me dreams
Of the beautiful Annabel Lee;
And the stars never rise, but I see the bright eyes
Of the beautiful Annabel Lee:
And so, all the night tide, I lie down by her side
Oh my darling – my darling – my life and my bride,
In her sepulchre there by the sea –
In her <u>tomb</u> by the sounding sea.

Tears filled Aaron's eyes. He started to cry uncontrollably. Rachael, dear Rachael was his new Annabel Lee.

As he wiped away the tears, he glanced at the jacket on the coffee table. He noticed the breast pocket was turned to the outside and the old, partially torn, slightly yellowed newspaper clipping given to him by Arturo was sticking part way out.

Aaron leaned forward and pulled the clipping out of the breast pocket. He thought back to Arturo Bandini and how he had died. He gently unfolded the clipping, being careful not to tear the old paper. He saw that there was a picture on the back side that he had not observed when he was reading it in Arturo Bandini's home.

He noticed it was a picture of the Hopkins family. The headline above it read that the picture was taken approximately one year before the murders and suicide in Hopkins House. Not paying too much attention to the picture itself, Aaron read the caption below it.

The caption read: *Pictured above from left to right are Harry, Anna, Candace, Charlene and Rachael Lynn Hopkins.*

Aaron stared at the picture, and the woman on the end appeared to get bigger in his mind. The picture seemed to pulsate and jump out at him. Oh no, oh no, Rachael, dear Rachael, was a ghost.

THE END

DO NOT READ BEFORE FINISHING THE BOOK

Listed below are the clues the reader should have picked up as indication of what Aaron would find out in the end.

THE CLUES TO THE ENDING

Page 21, Rachael says that ghosts would not announce themselves.

Page 30, the money she used was old and tattered.

Page 33, the silk blouse and orb-like breasts are the same descriptions as used previously for Rachael.

Page 34, the description of the younger sister was the same as Rachael's description.

Page 60, just one of several times when Rachael refuses food.

Page 61, Rachael is in period costume in the photo.

Page 65, she appeared to not be breathing.

Page 67, she says, "Ghosts are as real as you and I."

Page 68, there is another description of the younger sister's breasts that parallels the way Rachael's are described.

Page 69, Rachael looks forlornly at the spot where the younger sister died.

Page 91, Rachael says that there is something that will forever keep them apart.

Page 95, Aaron turns his back, and Rachael leaves the room as if she disappeared into thin air.

Page 104, in the evil room, the shadow of a woman appears and Aaron feels love.

Page 107, shadow of the woman and the smell of the lilacs is in the room. Lilacs represent the aforementioned smell of Rachael which was described earlier in the book.

Page 108, like many other times, Rachael is only present at night.

Page 118, Arturo Bandini hints that the entire Hopkins family in New York died out with the massacre in Hopkins House.

Page 129, as mentioned at other times, Rachael's hands are cold, indicating that she is dead. Also, she mentions that she has not left the house in years, which indicates she is trapped there as a ghost.

A PERSONAL NOTE ON THE HOPKINS CONNECTION FROM THE AUTHOR

As a child, I spent many happy times with my relatives who were descendents of Mark Hopkins. My great grandmother was a Hopkins, and I fondly recall as a small child, the times I would play in my sandbox while she sat in a rocking chair, watching me. In fact, I refused to eat my peanut butter and crackers unless she made them for me. Nobody could make them that special way but her.

In the ensuing years, I have never forgotten the gentle, serene way she went about showing love for me and the rest of her family. My grandmother, Vada Frye and my aunt, Willa Mae Cagle, no doubt, inherited the special "compassionate love" gene from this truly remarkable woman.

Although Harry Hopkins is a purely fictional character, Mark Hopkins is not. There were two Mark Hopkins, just as this book relates, as it appears that there were often conflicting stories about the New York Hopkins and the North Carolina Hopkins. Ironically, both men did show up in California at almost the same time.

I can remember when I was a child attending Hopkins Reunions in North Carolina, with hundreds in attendance, and listening to the lively discussions about our relative Mark Hopkins. Of course, the conversation always got around to all of us one day "cashing in" on the vast fortune that he left. Unfortunately, the New York Hopkins relatives were probably discussing the same thing. Neither Hopkins' family likely stopped to think that if the fortune was divided up among the then hundreds, and now thousands of descendents, we would all probably get a couple of thousand dollars each. Nonetheless, it was great fun to think about the possibility that we might all one day receive a great largesse from a long dead relative.

No matter how many stories were told, or how many times we thought about the money that might one day come our way, my favourite account of the saga was that Mark and Moses Hopkins high-tailed it out of North Carolina to escape from charges of horse thievery. There is just something about my penchant for fighting the establishment and flaunting authority that makes me swell with pride to know that I might be a descendant of a rogue rather than just a plain old millionaire.

J. Wayne Frye